"Tom Newton shows us how
extraordinary the ordinary is....
He gives ideas the charisma of actors."

—Djelloul Marbrook
award-winning poet / novelist,
Far from Algiers, The Light Piercing Water Trilogy

"The paired surrealist novellas in the aptly-titled *Voyages to Nowhere* masterfully explore the lacunae that divide being and experience. Tom Newton's vivid prose and striking imagery chart the brutal intersections between reality and imagination (or is it madness and sanity?) on a psychological, political and artistic level."

—Erica Obey, Ph.D.
award-winning author of
The Curse of the Braddock Brides, The Horseman's Word and *Dazzlepaint*.
President, New York Chapter,
Mystery Writers of America

VOYAGES TO NOWHERE

~ Two Novellas ~

REVOLUTION IN DREAMTIME

WARFILM

TOM NEWTON

VOYAGES TO NOWHERE

Two Novellas

This is a work of fiction. Names, characters, businesses, places, events and incidents are either the products of the author's imagination or used in a fictitious manner. Any resemblance to actual persons, living or dead, or actual events, is purely coincidental.

ISBN: 978-1-7337464-4-1
Library of Congress Control Number: 2021930663

Recital Publishing
Woodstock, NY
www.recitalpublishing.com

Cover painting: *Seascape* by Gorki Bollar, 1973
Cover design by Bryan Maloney

Extract page 90 from *The First Surrealist Manifesto* (1924) by André Breton. From *André Breton: Manifestoes of Surrealism*, trans. Richard Seaver and Helen R. Lane, (Ann Arbor: University of Michigan Press, 1969). Copyright © 1969, University of Michigan Press. Photo page 108: Wikimedia Commons / Bundesarchiv, Bild 183-1990-1002-500/CC-BY-SA 3.0. Photo page 228 by Dudley Newton, author's private collection.

An earlier version of *Warfilm* was published in 2015 as an ebook by Bloomsbury London.

Extracts from both *Revolution in Dreamtime* and *Warfilm* have appeared in audio and text on The Strange Recital podcast.

Recital Publishing is an imprint of the online podcast The Strange Recital. Fiction that questions the nature of reality
www.thestrangerecital.com

For Stefia

VOYAGES TO NOWHERE

REVOLUTION IN DREAMTIME

A Novella

"One has to be careful what one takes
when one goes away forever."

Leonora Carrington

1

Just before six o'clock in the morning, the old man leant his bicycle carefully against the wall. Not expecting satisfaction from life, he never found any and was always in a bad mood. If the bicycle fell it would make matters worse. A steady cold drizzle had been coming down for hours. He scanned the street for number seventy-one. He knew exactly where it was but he looked anyway. He did it every day. The quotidian bicycle trip halfway across Paris at an hour when it was more natural to sleep, only further exacerbated his grumpiness. All this was for one client who consistently underpaid him—a young woman who lacked the self-discipline to wake herself up in the morning.

He pulled his tricorn hat firmly down on his wig and unstrapped the bell. He stood outside number seventy-one and raised his arm. The three leopards inside the room had awoken at his approach, and at the first peal sprang from the bed and rushed snarling to the door. Sophia lay awake, feeling the coldness of the room on her face. She cooed to the leopards to calm them but they paid her no attention. The bell was ringing incessantly like knives in her ears. Finally, she propped herself up on one elbow and yelled out:

"All right, all right, I'm awake now. Can you please be quiet and go away!"

There were three more clangs, some clinking and then silence.

No bald Samoan strongman would ever arrive on hot summer nights to stand at the foot of her bed and cool her, his hefty arms cranking a large steel fan, which might squeak once in the same place at every revolution. There were no leopards, nor a bell ringer.

These were phantasmagoria—exercises of the imagination, which must be worked like a muscle for the world to blossom.

She slipped out of bed and pulled on a dress. She heated some water in a saucepan and poured it into the sink, quickly scooping it up by hand and washing the night from her face. She straightened her head and looked at herself in the blotchy mirror, then she darkened her eyebrows with charcoal.

Outside in the street, it was cold and damp. The fine wind-driven rain needled her exposed flesh. It was a foul day but it didn't bother her, as she was alive with inspiration, distracted by the excitement she always felt when about to start something new. She was headed to the studio she shared with Alphonse, and to the blank canvas awaiting her.

She would stop for coffee and a brioche on the way but first she would visit The Bureau, on the Rue de Grenelle. It was on her instigation that this establishment boasted a lectern with eagle-clawed feet and a giant blank tome—an oneiric catalogue available to anyone who wished to gaze at the invisible, or to contribute. She would map the subconscious. Sometimes she read, sometimes she wrote. She checked on it often.

Today she would write. She hauled up the chain with pencil attached.

"I am living in a large modern house. I wake up in the middle of the night and come downstairs to find that I have many more dogs than I previously imagined. Five or six of them are outside the glass door, harrying an animal that looks like a badger. On closer inspection, I see that the badger is in fact a very small, thin man, dressed in nothing but a loin cloth, who desperately wants to come inside. I begin to open the door and he attempts to get through, but I suspect his motives and close it again abruptly, trapping his head between door and frame. Then I take pity on him and open it again. He rushes in. He is begging me for something but I am not sure if I can trust him, so I pick him up and hang him from a hook on a coatrack. As soon as he finds himself hanging up there, he says he has changed his mind. I take him down and let him out of the door. He runs off into the night."

She let the pencil fall and bounce on its tether. Breton's idea of creating a new reality was very appealing. It promised freedom from that drab, turning wheel of servitude and disenchantment which constituted life for most people, a life of suffering and hopelessness. She admired Breton for what he had set out to do. As far as she was concerned it had all started with Dada. That was when the first cracks had begun to appear in the shell of consciousness. She had recognized it at the time and made sure she was a part of it, running off to Zurich and making an army of puppets, while the armies of Europe were destroying themselves in the trenches. Then it had all burst apart and, as the description went, rained down its spores on to a bed of fungus, from which sprouted Surrealism where she now found herself. It had provided a purpose—a direction that was no direction, a kind of rippling perfection. She was unable to differentiate her excitement about her place in the world from the picture she was about to paint. There was no need. They were the same thing.

The purists believed that artists should have no conscious engagement with what they produced. They were quite strident and vocal about it. Anything that had been consciously created was worthless. She disagreed with them. Such opinions seemed to her just another set of rules. Fundamentalism was unattractive in any guise. She would not be shackled. Thinking about what she was going to do before she did it, allowed her to focus her energies and put her in a place where something could bubble up through her, akin to the Pythia at the Delphic Oracle. Probably none of these purists created as autonomously as they would have people believe anyway.

Her mind, which seemed to have a mind of its own and was never quiet when she walked, took a momentary breath when she stepped onto the *Pont Neuf*—the old bridge, each arch an eyebrow. Crossing it was a symbolic act. All bridges were symbols and all symbols were bridges. That was symmetry. The studio was getting closer. The Métro would have been quicker but to reach a destination in the shortest time possible was never an important objective for her, and she wanted to walk. She would stop for coffee when she had passed the island where Jacques de Molay had been burned.

Often the shapes and movements of clouds would stimulate her imagination and she looked up to the sky. There were no discernible clouds, just an homogenous field of grey, so she looked down into a puddle of rainwater. Then she realized that she would paint a portrait. In her faint reflection she envisioned a Turkish man.

As a flake of stale brioche softened in her black coffee, the painting began to form. He stood in front of a large disc, his feet cropped by the edge of the canvas. A cavalry sabre hung from his right hip. He wore a blue uniform in the Napoleonic style. Two epaulettes perched on his shoulders, twin sunsets over a decaying empire, with greasy yellow, threadbare tassels. He had a narrow black moustache and a scarred face. He was most likely a survivor of smallpox. There was also a thin scar on his cheek that he might have received in a duel. He wore a fez.

Though her compositional technique did not conform to the automatism of those purists, she was finding her own way to the same place. The point where opposites were unified, that Hegelian idea Breton was always going on about, a kind of poetic explosion that would release enough force to sunder reality.

Breton had invited her into the group when they first met at a restaurant, and had instantly given her a title—Surrealist in the All-at-Once. She liked its metaphorical significance and the way it sounded. It felt good to be accepted. He wasn't known to be so welcoming and she suspected that the fact that she had arrived at the restaurant completely naked might have had something to do with it. None of them could resist uninhibited nubility. Despite their brilliance and open-mindedness they still exhibited certain masculine clichés, of which they did not seem to be aware. That was part of the problem. So be it. They certainly did not appreciate crones, except perhaps, Devereux.

Her hand reached for the doorknob of the studio, when she heard Alphonse talking and then a staccato reply. It could only be Nudreski. She had not seen him for months. He had been in Mexico recuperating from a surfeit of opium and alcohol. He must have just returned. Nudreski was the son of a tsarist diplomat. His mother had died in childbirth and his father had been mostly absent, posted overseas. He was brought up by wet-nurses, governesses, servants and tutors, until at the age of eighteen he had burst into St. Petersburg and never returned. As his allowance dwindled from a trickle to a drip, his life devolved into gonorrhoea and jars of laudanum. He was left with nothing but a profound hatred of everything. That's the way he told it, though you had to take whatever he said with a pinch of salt.

When she entered, he was staggering back from Alphonse's paintings with a half-drunk bottle of wine in his hand.

"Shit. Pure shit." He turned as he heard her in the doorway.

Nudreski had pushed hedonism over the crest of pleasure, but still had a physical vigour surprising in someone so debauched. She thought his body must be held together by the force of his personality alone.

"Anyone can paint."

He let the monocle drop from his eye.

"Only the bourgeoisie make a religion out of it."

When she was younger she might have been interested in a man like him—for his extremism, his drunkenness or his cultured nihilism. Now she saw him as a parasite, preying on artists younger than himself, doing the rounds, getting handouts and insulting the people who helped him, just managing to survive on a reputation that perhaps had always been false and was definitely worn thin, and he was only getting worse. He was excruciating. An encounter with him was like a meeting with death.

She went to Alphonse's aid.

"Most artists and revolutionaries come from the bourgeoisie. They are the only ones with the education and the time."

Nudreski violently swung his head and turned his combative attention to her.

"They're animals. All of them. Dogs, monkeys and parrots. Take your pick."

That kind of senseless denigration of animals infuriated her. What made humans assume they weren't animals? And what kind of animal was he? But there was no point getting drawn in.

Meanwhile Nudreski had turned back to Alphonse and was swigging more wine.

"Artifice!"

He waved the bottle at a painting Alphonse had been working on.

"There are people in prison for less than this."

Alphonse stood by, somber and silent. Nudreski continued unabashed.

"If you have the gall to create art, then at least make fetishes. No pretense there, just blood, bone and shit. And maybe some feathers."

He finished off the bottle and hurled it through the window, shattering the pane. Alphonse seemed suddenly to inflate.

"Get out!"

It felt as if Nudreski had taken all the oxygen with him when he left. They stood in a vacuum, her inspiration had withered and Alphonse looked depressed.

"I don't know why I keep letting him in here. I feel like putting my feet through these paintings."

"I know. He's suffocating"

"Maybe he has a function in the bigger scheme of things. A negative function. He's a tonic for self-delusion. It makes me wonder what I'm doing. You know... the surrealists won't let me in. Not that I want them to. But rejection is rejection."

"It's all politics. Don't let it bring you down. You're from Brittany. There's your way in. Let's go out and eat something. I'm going to see Josephine Baker later. She's at the Casino de Paris. After that I'm going to a performance by Devereux at his new place. Why don't you come with me?"

Alphonse was somewhere else. He remembered those eyes staring down into his, just after dawn. One brown, one green. If there was such a thing as fate, it had a bitter taste. He would have liked to go with her but there was something else he had to do.

Slivers of glass lay on the windowsill, and on the floor below it. The violence was still present.

"No, you go. I'll stay here and clean up."

2

Ferdinand always dined alone. He liked it that way. He never had to waste his time on idle chatter, which left him free to observe the people around him and listen to what they were saying. Sometimes he gleaned worthwhile information but mostly he just improved his understanding of humanity—a kind of general knowledge that usually confirmed his opinions. There was always a lot of talk about relationships. He found it both boring and fascinating. It was useful too, because manipulation required comprehension.

He had never entered into any kind of relationship himself, despite the nagging entreaties of his mother. He had acquaintances and associates—the usual necessities of work, but he didn't care for them personally. His dealings with people revolved around who was useful to him, and who was not. Of course he had desires—animal desires, mindless and base. These he would assuage late at night with a variety of prostitutes. It was convenient and never involved him in the delusion of love. With their anonymity and promiscuity, their drug addictions and their need for cash, prostitutes were ideal.

He ate out every night except on Sundays, never visiting the same restaurant twice in any given week. He knew that routines were careless but this one seemed harmless enough, as long as he stayed alert. Besides, there was no one to cook for him and he would not consider doing it himself. He abhorred domesticity of any kind. By fudging some numbers he was able to write off the cost of most meals as business expenses, incurred in the line of duty. He was a policeman—plain clothes. Any questions about veracity could be nipped in the bud. He always made sure he knew too much.

He arrived thirty-five minutes before the time he had arranged to meet Alphonse. He was always early to meetings, like the hunter setting his trap. It gave him the pleasure of anticipation.

He ordered sautéed chicken and a glass of Sancerre, then let his eyes rove across the room. Gluttony and gossip surrounded him. He was repulsed by how so many of these people had allowed their bodies to deteriorate. It wasn't just the bodies but also the clothing. For his age he was in excellent condition, with a fine physique and razor sharp acuity, and he took great care with his appearance. This bovine mass had no self-control, they were stupid and powerless, waiting to be herded. They inspired in him a low grade anger that he kept in check but sometimes expressed as annoyance.

When his food arrived he picked at it slowly and took small sips from his glass. He wanted to draw out his meal, making it last until Alphonse had finished eating, then he would catch him outside. It would not do for them to be seen together. But Alphonse had not yet arrived. He looked at his watch. He could not tolerate tardiness. It wasn't just because he disapproved of it, but because he was being flouted. A guffaw of laughter from the next table interrupted his thoughts. He ran his hand across his cheek; the scar was itching. That Vietnamese boy had surprised him with his hidden knife. He had made a rare but inadmissible error that night.

As he lowered his hand he saw Alphonse walk past his table to the other end of the room.

There was a joy to watching people unawares and an equal joy observing those who knew they were being watched. He glanced over to Alphonse frequently and caught his eye. The knowledge between them, with no words spoken, created a delightful tension.

When Alphonse was getting near the bottom of his soup bowl and his second glass was empty, Ferdinand signaled the waiter.

"*L'addition s'il vous plait.*"

He paid and went out to the street. He left his wine two thirds full on the table, having stirred some salt into it. A scullion in the kitchen was bound to drink it. That would teach him.

Alphonse came out not long after him. Ferdinand was standing by a pool of light, smoking one of his Sobranie cigarettes.

"Let's walk."

"Nudreski is back."

Ferdinand knew that already.

"Since when?"

"I don't know. But it's recent. He just paid me a visit."

"You don't seem thrilled."

Alphonse had a classically Gallic profile, which Ferdinand found pleasing to look at.

"It wasn't a joyful experience."

"What about that girl you share the studio with?"

"What about her?"

"Is she a joyful experience?"

"You disgust me."

"Don't be so prudish. It's unbecoming for a surrealist."

"I'm not a surrealist."

"It's time you were."

It was easy to anger Alphonse and he enjoyed it, so he kept going.

"Give me something about her. Are you sleeping with her? What does she do? Where does she go?"

Alphonse was visibly upset. Ferdinand knew he had hit a nerve.

"We don't have any kind of relationship. We share a studio. You know that. She's a painter and she's gone to the Casino de Paris to see Josephine Baker. She likes her. Is that enough?"

"And what do you know about the headless man?"

"I don't know him."

"Don't try to be funny. You'll regret it."

They were walking along a footpath on the embankment near Le Pont de la Tournelle. It was late. There was no one else in sight. The dark water flowed quietly beside them. Ferdinand realized he was walking on the side closest to the river and it occurred to him that Alphonse might try to throw him in. He was younger, stronger and bigger. He definitely had a motive and there would be no witnesses, so he stopped to light another cigarette and when he resumed walking he made sure he was on Alphonse's left, away from the river's edge. He didn't really believe Alphonse had the will for such an act. He was a coward at heart, despite his wartime experiences.

"You know what I'm talking about—*Acéphale*. Georges Bataille and his friends. They have lots of fun in the Bois du Boulogne at night."

Alphonse stayed mute. He was looking at Ferdinand's shadow and was wondering what kind of being in the fourth dimension would project such a man in the third, who cast this shadow in the second.

"You will worm your way into the headless man, Alphonse, and then we will talk again. I shall look forward to it."

3

Sophia parted the curtains of maroon velour and ducked into the room. This was Devereux's new venue. She was greeted on the other side by Françoise, whose stout hand proffered a glass of hot tea. Sophia was familiar with this tea. It was brewed from a blend of black leaves and mushrooms, picked under the light of the full moon by Françoise's gnarled fingers, somewhere outside Paris, or so it was said. It had an hallucinogenic quality, which enhanced the procedures. She held the glass in both hands to warm them. Françoise sat on a stool by the entrance, a samovar beside her, dosing the guests as they arrived. Sophia thanked her and would have talked more but Françoise was extremely taciturn. She must have been in her eighties, an old peasant woman with crab-apple cheeks and intelligent eyes. Her relationship with Devereux was unclear. They were rumoured to be lovers.

Jean Claude Devereux had the confidence and good looks of a film star, but instead of a career on the screen, he chose to perform occult rituals. He was very charismatic. She really did not know him. No one did, but everyone knew of him. He was notoriously reclusive and mysterious. It was impossible to know whether he actually believed in the magical rituals he conducted, or if he was just making a performance out of them for some enigmatic reason of his own. But it didn't matter to her. She liked ambiguity. It gave a greater freedom to the imagination. Equally curious was how he had managed to get hold of this disused wine warehouse in Bercy. There would be no answers. She would not even bother to ask. It was definitely an improvement on his old cramped quarters.

Sophia moved into the room, which was filling with people who chatted quietly in small groups. Some were sitting in the folding chairs. Others stood. There were loners too, hovering at the edges. She took a few sips of tea, still holding the glass with both hands. It was as earthy and bitter as she remembered, maybe even more so. The only sources of light were candles in sconces on the walls. They flickered in the otherwise imperceptible draughts, throwing shadows which expanded and contracted.

She looked around and noticed someone on the periphery. He seemed to be taking an interest in her. What struck her about him was that he resembled the Turkish man whose portrait she had yet to paint. He did not have the uniform, or the pockmarked face, but he did have a thin scar on his cheek and bore an uncanny likeness to the man she had imagined. There was something deeply unpleasant about him. He had a glass of tea in his hand but he was not drinking it. She turned away to avoid him.

"Sophia."

Kurt approached her, looking earnest in his wire-rimmed glasses. It was a relief to see someone she knew.

"I've finished your coat of arms. If you come to my studio I'll show you. I think you'll be pleased."

"Thank you. What is it like?"

"Azure, three leopards passant in pale or, fesse engrailed gules with wyvern sinople thereon."

She was beginning to feel uncomfortable. It might have been Kurt's intensity, or the mushroom tea, or a combination of both. She was hot and felt as if there were insects crawling beneath her skin. Her eyes were drawn to the floor, which she could see in great detail despite the low light. It was narrow-boarded in a dry, splintery wood.

"To blazon, Sophia, is to give breath to an idea. It is the pneuma...."

Voices around them fell. Devereux was in the room. She was still looking at the floor and saw his feet first—Turkish slippers with pointed, curled toes like the fingernails of a madman. He wore a linen kaftan, belted at the waist, and an embroidered pillbox hat. He did not speak to his audience, or make any attempt to acknowledge them. He must have come through a curtain at the back of the room and picked his way through the scattered chairs to the area that had been prepared for the ritual. There was a circle painted on the floor and he stepped into it.

He walked the circumference slowly, pausing momentarily at each cardinal point. After completing the circle he stood in front of the table at the centre, avoiding the sigils painted on the floor. The table was narrow and draped with a damask of deep red. His thaumaturgical instruments rested upon it.

He raised his right arm and let his left hang at an angle from his body, and held that position for a long time. Sophia's neck was itching.

Eventually he let his arms drop and began to recite his incantation. He started very softly, as if muttering to himself, then without warning he suddenly exhaled violently through his nose, twice in rapid succession. It was a shocking sound. After that the incantation continued but this time projected into the room for all to hear. He had a deep and resonant voice that was beautifully rich. Sophia had no idea what language he was speaking so fluently. She had never heard anything like it. He delivered the words in a lilting tone and she could feel their cadence and rhythm in her body, as the rising and falling swell of an ocean.

He had taken the sword from the table and was making symbolic gestures with it, slashing the air as he walked backwards around the circle while he raised his incantation to a greater intensity. Sophia could feel the words pulsing in her temples. She was becoming nauseous and felt as if she might faint.

Devereux returned to the centre of the circle and held the sword blade down, both hands on the hilt. He had stopped talking. The room was eerily silent.

Then he took both hands from the sword and it remained floating in the air. Sophia was transfixed. The blood was pounding in her head. She saw nothing but the sword. Light seemed to be traveling up the blade through the hilt and out—a fountain of light. As she watched it, the sword became the leg of a woman, toes extended, hanging in the air. She thought she was about to lose consciousness. The heat was stifling. She had to leave.

She got up in a panic and crashed through the chairs, oblivious to everything except her need to escape. She rushed past the crone, who was saying something she did not understand.

Sophia calmed down a little when she was on the other side of the curtain. Her legs felt weak. Her surroundings were unfamiliar. This was not the way she had come in but she could not bring herself to go back into the main room. She saw an unlit passageway ahead of her, so she took it. At the end was another candlelit room, smaller than the first. There were no windows, just a solitary door of heavy mahogany, studded with bolts. At eye height, in the centre, was a short, loosely nailed plank. Squatting on the floor nearby was a man in a hooded leather jerkin. He looked like a blacksmith from an earlier time. His bare forearms rested casually on his thighs. She could feel the torsion in his muscles. He studied her calmly. She felt threatened.

"What are you doing here?"

He spoke slowly. She didn't know what to say but felt she had to justify herself.

"The old lady sent me. Why? What is this?"

"It's the way out."

She was feeling nervous but not panicked as before and the nausea had diminished.

"I could go back the way I came."

"You could, but if the old lady sent you, then it seems that it's already been decided."

"Do you work here?"

"In a manner of speaking."

"What do you do?"

"I send people across. Are you going?"

"Across where?"

"Look."

He jumped up with an unexpected nimbleness and swung back the plank on the door, holding it up for her.

"Go on."

She put her eye to the hole. She saw a large field of grass and a palatial building on the other side. It looked like an aristocratic estate of the *Ancien Régime*. She stepped back and he glanced through before letting the plank fall.

"You have to cross over the field and enter the building. There's a door opposite this one. It looks like they're between chukkers at the moment."

"What do you mean?"

"There are horsemen out there playing the King's game. They take three minute breaks between chukkers. It's as good a time to go as any."

He was unlocking the door as he spoke. It swung open towards the field. Cold air blew in.

"They might even be on half-time, if you're lucky."

He gave her a quick shove and she was outside on her own. The door swung shut.

She could see horses now. Four at each end of the field. She launched herself into a desperate sprint. She had no way of knowing when the game would resume and adrenalin took over. When she reached the middle she heard the pounding of hooves and the ball flew by her. Almost instantly she was surrounded by horses, and mallets wildly raining down. Instinctively she threw herself to the ground and curled up with her arms around her head. There were heaving bellies above, sinews, falling hooves, the sounds of grunting, shouting, snorting, the smell of broken turf and sweat. Then they were gone. She had just rolled over and got back on to her feet, when she felt a sudden pain in the side of her knee—she had been hit by the ball. It came to a rest next to her. But it wasn't a ball. It was a severed head. Nudreski's—bruised and beaten, missing an eye. Then the horsemen were upon her again. She saw the downward arc of a mallet, swung by a quilted man standing up in his stirrups. Before she was hit, another stick blocked the swing, and then another sent the head coursing through the sky. They were gone again.

There was a distant whooping. It seemed that a goal had been scored, and as the horsemen galloped to reverse their positions on the field, Sophia made it to the other side. When she knew she was safe, she sat down on the low retaining wall below the mansion, to rest and regather her composure.

She was muddied and there was blood on her knee. It did not take her long to find out that the blood was Nudreski's and not her own. She cleaned herself up as best she could with leaves and saliva. When she had finished, she rested a while longer. The entrance to the building was directly up from where she sat, just as the hooded man had said. She would have to cross a croquet court, which was fortunately inactive. She turned back to the field. The game had started again.

Sophia stood in front of the door and clanged the bell next to it. She waited. She heard nothing, except for the sounds coming up from the field. She rang again and put her ear to the door to listen for motion. There was a faint scraping noise, which was getting closer. Then the door opened partially and a breathless man in livery peered out at her. He opened it a little more, just wide enough to let her through.

"Welcome, Madame. All visitors must be announced. If you would please follow me."

She was in an anteroom. As the usher began to lead her to three marble steps, only a short distance away, she understood that he was barely able to walk. The effort obviously caused him a great deal of pain, his face was sweating. He needed assistance to climb the steps and put a clammy hand on her wrist.

"I am most dreadfully sorry, Madame."

When they finally reached the top, the announcer came out of a coat room. He was wearing the same livery, and inclined his head in a slight bow to Sophia. He was shorter and swarthier than the usher.

"If if Mm-Madame would b-be pleased to p-p-pro-provide her n-n-name."

"Sophia Villeneuve, Monsieur."

His dark eyes seemed to light up for a moment with a flicker of interest.

"M-m-m-might I ask if y-y-you are re-re-re-related to the admiral?"

"No. I don't think there's any connection."

The announcer turned, disappointed perhaps, and opened the tall double doors before them. Sophia followed them inside. They were standing at the top of a grand staircase. Below them was a room the size of a cathedral, its space divided by heavy Romanesque arches and pillars.

The announcer braced himself and took in a deep breath.

"Madame S-Ss-Ss-Ss-So-ph-phia Ville-ne-ne-ne-ne-ne-ne-ne-neuve."

With a grimace, the usher leaned over and spoke softly in her ear.

"Would I be impertinent to ask if Madame could possibly go down on her own?"

Sophia smiled in affirmation and descended the staircase. A giant cross hung from the vaulted ceiling. Inside it was a naked woman draped with a large cut of raw meat, from collarbone to pudendum. She seemed to hang above a bucolic landscape, a river meandering in the distance, a shaggy bison in the foreground below her. In the arms of the cross was an assortment of sausages, steaks and chunks of stewing beef. She paused on the step, it was a striking painting, impressively displayed.

There were people wandering in the great space below her. All of them were dressed in the clothing of the Renaissance, mostly in primary colours. At the bottom of the staircase was a group of women with covered heads, and a dwarf, who stood by a life-size statue of a cow, completely fashioned from vegetables and fruits. Pumpkins, radishes, bananas, squash, apples, grapes, potatoes, melons and tomatoes were tightly wired together. It reminded her of an anatomical diagram, the kind which showed the ligatures and internal organs of a body.

She had the impression that this was a museum or art gallery. She was just another visitor, alone and anonymous. The stuttered announcement of her name had seemed incongruous. Maybe it was a relic of a tradition with a forgotten purpose. Meaningless tradition was an interesting idea.

On the floor beyond the vegetable sculpture were three scorbutic beggars playing dice. Their ribs protruded and their legs were no thicker than their bones. They were naked except for the tattered cloths around their waists. Their skins were covered in open sores.

For some reason she did not understand, these beggars inspired her with the desire to be naked, and she discarded her clothes, throwing them down in a heap.

She walked deeper into the big room, past a large urn containing a sun dial. Then she saw two cowled monks, tucked into an alcove between columns. They seemed to be plotting something malignant and she moved over to the other side of the room to put distance between them. Her panic had subsided but now she felt depressed and very cold. She wondered what had made her throw away her clothes and thought perhaps that she should go back and retrieve them but she did not want to pass those monks again. They frightened her. She kept walking and soon came across another two men, who were clasping each other and whispering passionately. Their expressions of love made her feel better.

In the transept a man with a dog was looking at the plinth of a column. She stood beside him and followed his gaze to a classical scene of Orpheus coming up from the underworld.

"Excuse me Monsieur, can you tell me what this place is?"

"It is a charnel house, Madame."

"A charnel house?"

"That's the way I see it."

"I don't understand."

"You could perhaps say that it's a provincial railway station."

"It doesn't look like a station."

"I don't mean that literally. It's one of many similar places along a vast network that emanates from a hub—a kind of Central Station if you like."

"I really don't follow you."

"It's a metaphor. The network I'm talking about bears the units of culture—the stories, the myths, the religions, the images, the fashions—haven't you ever wondered where these things come from?

"I suppose I have."

"I'm curious how you can be ignorant of these things."

"So am I. But please tell me more. Does this place have a name?"

"Absolutely not. No names. And that's by design. The work we do here is secret, and what I just described as a Central Station is even more secret still."

"Why the secrecy?"

As they talked she had the growing desire for casual sex.

"If all this wasn't secret you'd have every jackass and his cousin trying to interfere. It would be mayhem. It's mad enough as it is. There's a lot of regulation involved. More than you might think."

"So what exactly is this Central Station?"

"It's rather like a library and factory rolled into one. A vast machine really, operated by a skeleton crew. This is where the goods are made, then they are shipped out along the network. But there's back and forth—some come back for readjustment before being sent out again. It's a perpetual process."

"But who runs it? Can you go there?"

"It is shrouded in such a deep level of secrecy that no one really knows, but there are rumours. They say the whole system is overseen by a Doge. Whether that's a name or a title I don't know. And then there are a handful of guards or operators. But as it is a kind of machine, I suspect that it basically runs itself. No one ever goes there. No one knows where it is."

"Why are you telling me this, if it is such a big secret?"

"Because I'm disillusioned and I need to unburden myself. We deal with some beautiful things here but we also peddle in brutality and ignorance. Sometimes I think that all we really accomplish is to perpetuate suffering. It doesn't sit well on my conscience. There needs to be some radical change. But that will never happen."

Sophia knew what she was going to do.

She looked up at the man standing next to her. He had a skirted coat of golden ochre, tight black trousers tucked into knee high boots, a sword on his belt and a black hat with the brim turned up at the front. She liked the clothes people wore in this place.

"Would you be interested in having sex?"

"Where?"

"Right here."

It took several minutes for him to remove his codpiece. It was an intricate affair. Sophia leant back against a sarcophagus.

The black dog licked her ankle.

4

Ferdinand got home very late. The night had been a disaster. He had come back without his jacket or his shoes like some common tramp. It had been dark and he couldn't spend the time to look for them in his haste to leave. At least he had been able to find his trousers and shirt. Devereux had humiliated him in the worst possible way in front of a roomful of people. He could not understand how he had allowed this to happen. He felt as if he was not the person he supposed himself to be. He could barely stand to think about it. There would be a high price to pay for this.

Ferdinand pulled out a chair and sat at his desk. He must have been drugged. That would explain it. The old witch had probably spiked his tea. The trouble had started with Sophia Villeneuve. She seemed to look right into him. Perhaps that was what excited him about her. She was a challenge. He wondered what had made her leave in such a hurry. But it was a good thing she hadn't witnessed what happened later.

He reached into his pocket and took out the scrap of paper the old woman had thrust into his hand as he left. He unfolded it and spread it on his desk, smoothing it with his fingers. It was a hand-written note that resembled a poem from the arrangement of the lines, except that it was written in gibberish.

Aq nuar geqv ne riea gaq runofoit
xe wait ni tavvi iw piwwti ni hia e retov.
Ni fkeqweji iw nurrtivvouq vuqw givotv tiprnefiv.
nepuat iw ne wtekovuq vuqw ne pipi fkuvi ruat nao.

He studied the handwriting carefully. It looked as if it had been written by a man. That meant the old woman was only delivering the message. It must have come from Devereux himself. Just the thought of that name made him wince.

Most likely it was a coded message that he was meant to

decipher, so it should be easy enough. The puzzle was alluring and gave him some relief from his humiliation.

The simplest cypher he could think of was a substitution code where one letter was replaced with another. He took a blank sheet of paper from the desk drawer and wrote the alphabet down the left side, then he copied the first line on to the middle of the page.

Aq nuar geqv ne riea gaq runofoit.

He scanned the line looking for words that might represent the definite or indefinite article. That seemed a good place to start. If the coded language was French, which he presumed it was, then those would likely be '*aq*' or '*ne*'.

On a whim he picked the word 'ne'. If he was correct, it could mean '*le*', '*la*', or '*un*'. If it was the definite article, he would favour '*la*', because 'le' shared a vowel with '*ne*', and there would have been no substitution if those two letters matched. Against the '*L*' on the side of the page he wrote '*N*'. After that he wrote the letters sequentially, keying from the *L/N* link.

Decoding the first sentence using this key produced:

Yo lysp ecot lc pgcy eyo pslmdmgr.

It was obviously not the answer. He needed another key. He wrote out the new line of gibberish above the original.

Yo lysp ecot lc pgcy eyo pslmdmgr.

Aq nuar gekv ne riea gaq runofoit.

Comparing the two lines, he saw that the original had thirteen vowels, while the other contained only five. This might very well have no significance, but his intuition told him that it did. What if Devereux had used two keys—one for consonants and one for vowels? He followed his hunch and rewrote the letter correspondence in two new columns, using the same key but omitting the vowels in both. This produced:

Aq nuar geqv ne riea gaq runofoit.

-n l--p d-ns l- p--- d-n p-l-c--r

As he assumed that 'ne' could be the female definite article, he entered the letter '*A*' for every incidence of '*E*'.

-n l--p dans la p-a- d-n p-l-c--r.

This was beginning to look like French. He wrote the vowels in one line and their substitutions in another line below, assuming the coded 'E' vowel must be 'A' and using the same direct sequence as he had for the consonants:

E I O U A

A E I O U

This gave him:

Un loup dans la peau d'un policier.

Now he had it, and with a rush of excitement he quickly decoded the rest.

Un loup dans la peau d'un policier
va tuer le Russe et mettre le feu à Paris.
Le chantage et l'oppression sont désirs remplacés,
l'amour et la trahison sont la même chose pour lui.

(A wolf in the skin of a policeman
will kill the Russian and set fire to Paris.
Blackmail and oppression are replaced desires,
love and betrayal are the same thing for him.)

He leaned back in satisfaction. That had been easy. It was very much the work of an amateur. The sequences should have been more jumbled. Then he remembered that the cypher was meant to be broken. It sounded like a quatrain by Nostradamus, just the kind of affectation he might expect from someone like Devereux.

He of course, was the wolf in the skin of a policeman—a little hyperbolic but not unfitting, and the Russian was obviously Nudreski. That man had been a disappointment from the start. He had become a liability. His desperate need for money had made him ripe for the plucking but his advanced alcoholism caused him to be impervious to reality. His information was unreliable at best. When he had made that befuddled attempt at blackmail, he had taken it too far.

The question was, how much did Devereux know? How did he know it and when?

The use of the future tense in the quatrain made that unclear. Perhaps that was his intention. He was covering his tracks by being deliberately vague.

It could only have been Sophia who had led him to Bercy. He had followed her from the Casino de Paris, curious to see where she would go. He thought he had been trailing her, not being led. If she was involved, then Alphonse was too. This was a plot against him.

He looked again at the note on the desk. Devereux had intended him to decipher it, so he was meant to know about the plot against him. What was the point of that? Was it a ruse to hide a deeper conspiracy? He was being outmanoeuvred and put on the defensive. Sophia and Alphonse were easy enough to deal with, but he feared that in Devereux he might finally have met his match.

The last two lines about replaced desires, and love and betrayal seemed merely to be intended as an insult and were just fluff—something to conclude the rhyme, but the reference to burning down Paris was more interesting.

Ferdinand reached in to the back of the drawer and felt around for his ball of opium. Then he sat down on the bed and prepared himself a pipe. It wouldn't help him sleep but it would alleviate the effects of his perpetual insomnia and his worries. He lay back and drew in the smoke, holding it in his lungs a moment before exhaling.

Thinking about the code again, it suddenly came to him that Devereux had used the first two letters of his last name for the two keys. Of course, that was his signature.

Perhaps Devereux actually was the prophet he pretended to be.

5

He awoke with a start to see the silhouette of a woman beside him.

"Sophia, is that you?"

"I'm cold. Can I get in bed with you?"

He pulled back the covers to let her in, and almost yelled from the shock of her naked back touching his stomach.

"What's going on?"

She was already asleep, gently snoring, and didn't answer.

In the morning they went out and ate breakfast together. He had given her some of his clothes and she looked a little like Charlie Chaplain as she picked at her food in silence.

"What did you do with your clothes?"

"I don't know."

"It must have been quite a night."

"It was."

She was not her usual ebullient self and conversation was an effort, so Alphonse retreated into his own thoughts. After a few minutes she put down her coffee cup and pushed it away from her.

"Alphonse..."

"Yes?"

"I'm not going to paint anymore. I'm giving it up."

"Why? Does it have anything to do with Nudreski?"

"He's dead."

"Nudreski?"

"Yes. I saw his head on a polo field."

"Where were you?"

She didn't answer and he didn't press her. Something was definitely not right. Then she suddenly perked up.

"Can you imagine visiting your own mind as if it was a foreign country?"

He had never felt that way about his mind, but all the same, it was not an unreasonable question. She now seemed enlivened and didn't give him time to answer.

"That's where I've been. And I'm going back."

"How?"

She slipped back into thought.

"I don't know yet."

Alphonse pushed back his chair.

"Let's go. We can talk more in the studio."

"No. I'm going home. I'll tell you about it later."

Outside, as she started to walk away, she stopped and turned back to him.

"The tide has come in. It's earlier than usual."

He was worried about Sophia. She seemed quite different. He sat down on the floor and looked at *The Eye of the Impostor*—the painting he had been working on for more than a year, and the one that had warranted him a prison sentence according to Nudreski. He had mixed feelings about it, and had painted over sections again and again, never being satisfied. He could understand her doubts about painting. They were harder to get over without the momentum of public accolade. If she wanted to give up painting he would not try to dissuade her, and he would not allow himself to feel abandoned. Those kind of regrets spoke more about his own doubts.

He got up and turned the painting upside down and sat back to look. It was better this way. The balance of colour was radically altered and the image opened up. He saw new possibilities. Then he noticed something under the bed. He groped around and pulled out a deflated football. It had been stabbed with a kitchen knife that was still embedded in it.

This was as cruel a sight as he had ever seen, and he had seen bad things. It stopped his breath for a moment. He stared at the blade, imagining the force of its entry and found himself feeling sorry for the ball. Tired of the sight, he went into the other room.

Someone had broken in while they were having breakfast, which meant they were being watched. The first person who came to mind was Ferdinand.

He looked around carefully to see if anything had been stolen, but as far as he could tell the place was just as he had left it, except for the addition of the murdered ball. That seemed to rule out a break-in by a street urchin or petty thief. This was obviously a threat.

Ferdinand was perfectly capable of cruelty but he was fastidious in dress and walked with measured steps. He didn't seem like someone who would be prone to rash and impulsive actions. Unless he was desperate.

Alphonse had the feeling that things were closing in around him. He had to find a way to give Ferdinand some information about *Acéphale* without compromising anyone too badly. He didn't know Georges Bataille. He had heard that *Acéphale* was obsessed with human sacrifice but had come to an impasse because everyone wanted to be the victim and no one the killer. He didn't want to infiltrate the group and wasn't particularly interested in them. He never liked to get involved with anything that didn't interest him. Intelligent but undisciplined, a dreamer and a fritterer—that had been the opinion of his teachers when he was a boy. It was a criticism that still made him proud.

He would go and talk to Devereux. They weren't exactly friends but had been students together at L'Acadamie Julian. Devereux would have an opinion. But then the question arose as to how frank he should be. The life of an informant was a hollow affair. He had suffered a generational trauma and now this. The best thing would be to disappear, somewhere far away.

Alphonse gathered some newspaper and wrapped up the ball. He took it outside and threw it away. Then he dabbled with his painting for a while but did not feel inspired, so he lay down on his bed and was soon asleep.

"Alphonse."

It was Sophia, waking him up for the second time that day.

"I owe you an explanation."

"You do?"

"Yes, I..."

"Hold on a minute. I've got to wake up."

He got out of bed and poured himself a glass of wine. He poured one for her too. She seemed her normal self again.

"You were saying..."

"I said I was giving up painting but that doesn't mean I will cease being an artist. I'm just changing my focus to something more multi-dimensional."

"Sculpture?"

"No."

She proceeded to tell him about her experiences of the previous night, and how the man she had met explained it to her.

"So you're talking about a network of ideas."

"Yes. All emanating from a Central Station and returning there like a railway network."

"But there is no Central Station in Paris."

"I'm not talking about Paris. The Central Station is a metaphor. Maybe 'Power Station' would be better."

"But where is it?

"I'm not sure. Most likely in the mind."

"Whose mind?"

"Everyone's. But don't confuse the brain with the mind. Brains are individual. Minds are not so bound. The mind to the brain is like walking to the leg. Minds are dynamic. They are imbued with culture. That's what makes reality. But where do those ideas come from? The Central Station—that's where. I'm going to find it and I'm going to make some changes. This will be the new reality that Breton is talking about. This kind of art leaves painting and sculpture behind. Don't you see it?"

"What about the senses? Don't they contribute to reality?"

"Yes but they are beholden to the brain and thus to the mind."

She was getting worked up and he was beginning to find it tiresome. He had never given much credence to Breton's idea of a new reality. Breton was a poet and it was a poetic idea. It was interesting, but what made it more real than the reality he wished to replace?

"So when are you going?"

"I don't know. I have to find a way to get there."

He had no wish to discourage her however futile he thought her quest but he couldn't prevent himself from expressing what he was thinking. It was an idea that had been brewing for a while.

"How tall are you?"

"Just over a metre and a half. Why?"

"I have this theory about the duration of relevance. I'm going for a stroll. If you're still here when I get back, we'll calculate how long your idea about the Central Station, or Power Station will remain relevant."

When he left the studio, he turned on to Rue des Saules and pulled the notebook from his pocket. The mural of a giant cowboy in a checked shirt, doffing his hat with one hand and raising his gun with the other, covered the wall of a corner building. It never failed to catch his eye.

The idea about the duration of relevance had come to him when he had been looking at his painting, before he had been distracted by the ball. Maybe he should call it 'Almost The Eye of The Impostor', as he liked the painting but had been having trouble with it recently. It occurred to him that there might be some kind of temporal relevance unique to artistic ideas, and in his case it had expired. It would be nice to find a way to determine this duration of relevance. How could he calculate the incalculable? Mathematics would seem the obvious answer but his knowledge was limited.

Three things seemed integral for such a calculation. He opened the book and started to write while walking.

1. The originator of the idea.
2. The number of other artistic ideas the originator is engaged with at the time the idea is conceived.
3. The possibility of a random occurrence which might affect the duration.

To represent the originator, take body mass (m) and height (h). Multiply to determine the originator quotient (q), then divide by the number of other ideas (n).
From this number, subtract the random number (θ).
The random number could be the street address of where the calculation is being carried out.
Divide the result by the age of the originator (a) to determine the temporal relevance of the idea (t).

So:

$t = \{(mh)/n\text{-}\theta\}/a$

t would be measured in units of days.
h would be tabulated in centimetres and m in kilograms.
a would always be measured in years.
For females, increase (mh) by 21% to compensate for mean sexual dimorphism.

Now he had the formula to determine the duration of relevance for his painting. It was a simple and stupid idea, but it was in stupidity that a grain of truth might present itself. He was excited as he began the calculation.

In his case q was 14,322.552. He had entertained two other artistic ideas in the course of the painting. One had involved projecting the shadows of trees on to barren landscapes, and the other a fireplace. So n was 2, and θ was 39, the address of the studio.

He ran the equation, t was 178.0569—almost six months. No wonder he was having trouble with this painting.

As he approached the studio he was thinking of Vivian, his secret lover and wife of the British Under Secretary. They had been carrying on an affair for over two years. She would be back in Paris soon.

When he got in, Sophia was still there. He lost little time to try out his new formula on her.

"So you say you are just over a metre and a half. I could measure you if you'd like."

There was a folding wooden ruler in the umbrella stand.

"No. I'm one metre sixty three."

"Weight and age?"

"Forty-four and a half kilos, and I'm thirty-one. You certainly know how to ask all the right questions."

"What about other artistic ideas? How many do you have going on?"

"None. This one wiped the slate clean."

"We'll make *n* one, and as we're doing the calculation here, the random number will be thirty-nine. So... let me see... You have almost nine and a half months to find your Central Station."

It was just about the length of gestation in humans. That was an interesting metaphor.

6

When he arrived at the warehouse, it was gone. There was a jagged gap between the two adjacent buildings. A tangled mass of rubble and charred wood littered the ground. The smell of fire lingered. This completely derailed his plans and he stood wondering what to do next. He had spent the Métro ride to Bercy having an imaginary conversation with Jean Claude, but now he didn't even know if he was alive. He had hoped to get some information about *Acéphale* that would placate Ferdinand without ensnaring anyone.

He looked around him. Life continued despite the catastrophe. Further down the street an old woman sat on a low stool with a sketch pad resting on her knees. Her head scarf flapped in the breeze. When he glanced down he saw that she was drawing the arched doorways across the street.

"What happened here, Madame?"

She did not look up. Her pencil kept moving on the paper.

"There was a fire."

"I can see that. When did it happen?"

"Last night."

"Was anybody hurt?"

"They pulled out two bodies."

It was morning. He had an obligatory meeting with Ferdinand. The customary envelope had been slipped under the door. It seemed too soon for another meeting. What was he expected to accomplish in such a short time? He had to be at the Grand Cascade in the Bois de Boulogne at 3:00 pm. That left five hours to fill.

He did not feel like going all the way back to the studio and decided to engage in some bibliomancy instead. It was a game he sometimes played when he felt indecisive. He would randomly select and open a book. The first words he read would be the message that chance produced. He wasn't looking for prophecy or advice but a jolt that would open him up to different thoughts. It was the same kind of experience he got from looking at paintings. He enjoyed such games. There was something beautifully mysterious about chance. It was the outward expression of the underlying mathematics to everything.

Alphonse spoke very little English, so he thought it would be amusing to dip into an English-language book. In that case he would go to Shakespeare and Company on Rue de l'Odeon.

On his way there he devised the system he would use to pick a title. Street addresses were on his mind since the formulation of the relevance equation. They were the perfect numbers to use. He would use them again. Shakespeare and Company was located at Rue l'Odeon 12, so he would pick the twelfth shelf he saw when he went inside. There were twenty-one letters in the name, which meant he would choose the twenty-first book. The question arose as to whether he should count from left to right, or right to left and if he should start at the top of the shelf or the bottom. He decided to start at the bottom and count right to left. It was the less expected way and was more likely to produce pure chance.

There was a man leaning against the wall by the door when he arrived. He had one hand in his pocket and the other on a cane. His legs were nonchalantly crossed. He wore very thick spectacles and looked vaguely familiar.

Ignoring him, Alphonse opened the door and went inside. It was quiet and faintly musty. He quickly found the twelfth shelf and started counting.

The twenty-first book was a slim volume—*Levels of Imperfection* by Tom Newton. *Les Niveaux d'Imperfection*—he liked the title. The shelf was tightly packed and he had a hard time getting a grip on the spine. When it came free he let it swing down so the pages would splay open, and then he brought it back up again in one continuous motion.

"Failure is life's chief asset..."

It had a pessimistic ring but he wasn't concerned with its meaning, and anyway he could not be sure if he had translated it correctly. But that did not matter to him either. What he wanted from it was an emotional response. He read it again, then squeezed the book back on the shelf. It gave him the feeling that Devereux had perished in the blaze and there was nothing he could do about it.

He went quickly through the shop and out into the street, without looking at any other books. The man by the doorway had gone. The air outside was invigorating. He had plenty of time, so he decided to walk to Montparnasse and get a glass of wine.

There were not many people in the Select, which suited his mood. It was still too early for *Les Quartiers*. He didn't rush his wine but let his mind wander, imagining an installation in a gallery. There would be a mask set into a wall. Viewers would perceive it as the inside of a face. They would step up and put their own faces into it. They could not help but to look through the eyes. There would be lenses on the eyes, different for left and right. Perhaps one would magnify and the other reduce. They would play tricks on the brain.

He sipped from his glass and looked around him. Then he noticed Vivian, sitting at a table across the room with a man he did not recognize, older and well dressed. She must have seen him too but they never acknowledged each other in public. It was convenient for both of them. He didn't like his private life on view and she had appearances to keep. She must be carrying on multiple affairs. It wasn't a surprise and it didn't bother him. It was mildly exciting to sit and watch her, knowing who she was, without having to act as if he did. He looked at his watch. It was time to go. He drained his glass and left the money on the table.

He was early for his rendezvous in the Bois de Boulogne. As

he sat down on the designated bench he looked around for Ferdinand, who usually arrived before him. Unexpectedly, he was not there. Alphonse got up and walked around. For want of a better idea, he decided to count the trees.

There were many.

Counting trees in a forest, man-made or otherwise, without marking them, was an almost impossible task. Their large number was confusing, and he became sidetracked by trying to identify the different types. Elms, cedars, lindens, hornbeams, beeches, and chestnuts. He was more interested in variety than number, and he quickly lost count.

When he returned to the bench, Ferdinand was waiting, with a folded newspaper in his lap.

"You're late."

"I was counting trees."

"The pastime of a fool. What do you have for me?"

"Regarding *Acéphale*? Not much. What do you expect? We only just met two days ago. I went to talk to Devereux but his warehouse has burned down."

"For an informant, you are remarkably uninformed. Devereux left the group months ago."

"Did you know about the fire?"

"Yes."

"What was the cause?"

"I don't know yet. An explosion in his athanor, I imagine. They're working on it."

Ferdinand leant back and grinned, in appreciation of his own humour.

"Was he in the building?"

"It seems that he was. Him and that old hag, but I'm supposed to be asking the questions, not you."

They lapsed into silence.

There were no mud spatters on Ferdinand's shoes, his worsted suit was impeccably pressed. His hat appeared to be brand new as always, but his face looked more haggard than usual and he seemed to be distracted, betrayed by the motion of his eyes.

"Interest in *Acéphale* has warmed up. You're a disappointment. I've been accommodating but I'm going to have to let you go soon. If you know what's good for you, go and talk to Georges Bataille directly. Stop trying to hoodwink me."

Alphonse sat at the other end of the bench, as far away from Ferdinand as possible.

"There has been a murder. In this park. Not far from here."

He tapped Le Figaro on his leg with a gloved hand.

"It wasn't Nudreski, was it?"

Ferdinand's face remained inexpressive but his body tensed almost imperceptibly. Alphonse immediately regretted the question.

"What makes you think it was Nudreski?"

"Nothing in particular. I was wondering, that's all. He just showed up in Paris again and now he seems to have disappeared."

Ferdinand turned away from him and looked out at the park.

"It's hard to determine who it is. Head, hands and feet have been removed. And the genitals as well. But it's male. That much we know."

"And why the interest in *Acéphale*?"

"Are you really such an idiot, Alphonse? Do I have to spell it out for you? There's a group that cavorts illegally at night in the Bois de Boulogne. Their name is 'The Headless Man'. Their primary concern is human sacrifice. A decapitated body is discovered in the area. Do you understand now? Is there anything else I can help you with?"

He stood up as he spoke and removed his gloves, slender things of soft chamois leather. He crushed them in one hand, and picked up the newspaper he had thrown down on the bench.

"You need to start delivering."

The meeting was over. Alphonse stayed where he was for a while until Ferdinand was out of sight.

The pressure had only increased his inertia.

7

He did not like Captain Dubois. Not that it mattered. The captain was a martinet. He was also vain. A few days at the front had ruined his appearance, something he irrationally blamed on his subordinates.

Alphonse was tired. His boots had been sodden for a long time and his feet were rotting. With any luck his condition would worsen.

Morning came like any other. Alphonse was awake, uncertain if he had slept. He could hear the lonely song of a bird as the sky filled with gloomy light and the few remaining splintered trees were revealed, beautiful as the skeletons of ghosts. There were still pleasures to be had. He drew on his cigarette.

Captain Dubois picked his way along the trench with careful steps.

"We're going over in six minutes."

His different coloured eyes were startling.

"Fix bayonets."

There was an ominous silence after the barrage, which had ended some twenty minutes earlier, just enough time for the German machine gun crews to get back into position. There were a few seconds to go. The captain climbed up on to the parapet—gun in one hand, watch in the other, a whistle between his teeth.

Alphonse looked at the men around him. They were huddled on the firing-step. No one talked. Then he looked up at Captain Dubois. Their eyes met and forged a bond. Dubois knew that this time Alphonse would refuse to go over. Alphonse knew that Dubois would shoot him.

The captain's hollow cheeks moved a little, as his teeth tightened on the whistle. Alphonse shouldered his rifle. Dubois' weapon was already raised. Alphonse felt his finger about to tighten on the trigger. The whistle was just about to sound, and then Dubois suddenly toppled forward into the trench, blood pouring from his head, the victim of a sniper's bullet.

After that, there was confusion and a momentary loss of purpose. Some of the men went over. Others, including Alphonse, stayed where they were. They were later charged with mutiny.

Alphonse was also charged with the attempted murder of an officer. He was imprisoned while awaiting his court martial and was visited by the chaplain a few times, which was an annoyance. It interrupted his daydreams in which he often lay on his stomach at the edge of a pond. He would watch damselflies and dragonflies, larvae twisting just below the surface, and insects skating across it, enthralled by this alien form of life coexisting with his own.

He was sentenced to death by firing squad. The irony was so great it did not seem real—to survive the war only to be killed for a crime that chance had forestalled. Knowing the time of his death was disorientating and reduced him to despondency, casting him adrift.

The day before the sentence was to be carried out, Alphonse had a visitor—a dapper man who said he was a police inspector. This man said that due to extenuating circumstances, his death sentence would be commuted to government service for an unspecified period of time. He would be required to do covert work as an informant. The choice was his: agree to these arrangements or face the firing squad. An immediate decision was required. "Sign here."

He presented no credentials and there was no way to tell if he actually was who he claimed to be but it was not a concern. If the life and freedom he had offered were real, and not just some cruel trick or desperate hallucination, Alphonse would have signed anything.

That was how he had first met Ferdinand.

He was released the next day and discharged from the army.

Ferdinand had given him an address in Paris, along with a key and a small amount of money, and told him to wait there until contacted.

"What am I supposed to do?"

"Re-acclimate yourself to civilian life. Look for work. Start painting. You want to be an artist, don't you?"

It took him two days to reach the apartment on Rue Tourlaque. By the time he arrived he was feeling feverish. He made a few attempts with the key before he got the door open. The apartment was completely empty. It consisted of three small rooms. There was a sink against the wall in the middle one, below a window overlooking the street. He was glad to find a bathroom. It was cramped but at least not a shared facility out in the hallway. By this time his teeth were chattering and he lay down on the floor, covering himself with his army coat, alternating between shivering and sweating.

He stayed there for almost a week. It was hard to gauge the passing of time, just light and darkness. Sometimes he would heave himself up to the sink and drink from the tap, then crumple back down again, drifting in and out of sleep. His head frequently ached. His thoughts were confused and he was unable to follow them. It was a state of dreaming where there were no dreams. Occasionally he wondered if he was talking to someone, and if that person was himself. His tongue felt thick and gummy, his mouth like the floor of a bird cage.

One day he got up to drink and realized he was hungry. He rummaged around and found he still had a little money, so he went out for something to eat.

It was chilly outside and he was still very weak. He walked until he saw a café. Over a cup of coffee and a *croque monsieur*, he learned that Germany had been defeated and the war was over. His food was free. The woman who served him told him it was a small token for the sacrifices he had made.

8

Ferdinand was holding a bunch of flowers when he visited Alphonse at 39 Rue Tourlaque. He had come by the week before, and knocked on the door. When there was no answer he had let himself in. Alphonse was lying delirious on the floor. Ferdinand nudged him with his foot but there was no conscious response. He only stayed a few minutes, fearing exposure to the rampant influenza pandemic and covered the door handle with his handkerchief as he left.

Now, as he stood outside the door again, he didn't know what to expect. The bouquet seemed absurd, so he propped it in a corner and gave the door a sharp rap. There was motion within and the door opened a crack. Alphonse was still alive.

"Are you going to let me in?"

Alphonse opened the door fully and stepped back to let him pass. Ferdinand had intended to set out the parameters of their relationship, and to explain the role Alphonse would play in rooting out bolsheviks and social degenerates. He would give his usual pretext—the government was concerned with the spread of Bolshevism due to the repatriation of troops disillusioned by the war. It was credible enough. Christianity had moved from Palestine with the Roman legions. All kinds of dangerous ideas came back with soldiers. It was a legitimate concern. But as he looked over Alphonse's gaunt shoulder into the empty room beyond, and breathed the stale air, his intentions lost their relevance.

Instead he pulled an envelope from his jacket and handed it to Alphonse.

"Here's some money. Consider it an advance on the work you'll be doing for me. Get some furniture. Set yourself up. This is a one-time payment. Don't assume you'll be getting more."

Alphonse held the envelope without opening it.

"Thank you. And what am I supposed to do for this?"

His face was drawn. He was wearing his army coat and nothing much else. He was a pathetic sight. Their proximity made Ferdinand uncomfortable. Alphonse seemed to be an embodiment of abject weakness—his condition, his predicament—yet Ferdinand had the impression of a furtive strength, cowering but resilient, and his contempt was tempered by desire.

"You will give me information."

"About what?"

Alphonse swayed slightly on his thin legs. His pallor was offset by the dark stubble on his chin.

"About whatever I like. You will spy on your friends."

Ferdinand had made sure to wear gloves this time. He had always recoiled from sickness of any kind.

"We will meet from time to time. Not here. You'll receive instructions about where and when. First, pull yourself together. You're going to have to pay me rent for this place. And don't get any ideas about moving, if you know what's good for you."

He straightened his jacket and turned to leave.

"I've made a considerable investment in you and I expect a return."

When the door closed behind him, he retrieved his bouquet.

"Leave the flowers on the table. The girl will find a vase."

At least she knew who he was today.

"How was your week, Mother?"

"The servants in this place are all second rate. Where were they recruited? From the prisons?"

"There are no servants here, Mother."

"Well they lack respect, whoever they are."

His mother had spent her formative years in Algeria as the daughter of a colonial official. The house had been full of servants. Sometimes when he visited she mistook him for a butler.

"What is it you do?"

"I'm a police officer, Mother."

"A policeman? You?"

She never bothered to hide her disdain. It made him feel like a child—just not her child. He could not understand why he came back each week. It was perhaps a morbid attraction. Ever since he could remember, his mother had retreated into a world of dubious fantasy. He had always been a reminder to her of everything she had hated about her life and she had done her best to avoid him, even when they lived together. Now she was his dependent. Perhaps that was what kept him coming back. He came here to savour his power and the reversal of their roles, knowing that the assistance he provided could be withdrawn at any time he chose.

"I thought you were a lawyer like your father."

It was true, his father had been a lawyer—a seedy backstreet lawyer, who had squandered whatever talent he might once have had through excessive drinking. He had been struck off and reduced to making a living from criminals and the dregs of society. Occasionally he was prone to fits of uncontrollable anger and violence. He was a lecher. Ferdinand had never liked either of his parents and assumed he was the product of rape—his pregnant mother coerced into marrying her abuser and then ostracised by her family. Her disinheritance had not precluded some family money from being provided for his education. They regarded him as an unfortunate unmentionable. He felt no particular gratitude for their generosity. It had only reinforced his opinion of himself. He was a prime mover, unencumbered by friendship or by the need for love.

His father had introduced him to the Parisian underworld. He had learned first hand of extortion, protection and prostitution. They were exciting possibilities but the introduction was to be short lived, as his father was convicted on racketeering charges and sentenced to seven years hard labour in the penal colony Bagne de Cayenne. His sentence was mandatorily subject to the *doublage*—when he had done his time, he would have to spend another seven years in the colony. He never returned. Ferdinand was left to his own devices in the underworld. What better way to reap its benefits than to become a policeman?

"My work is to protect society, not to engage in sophistry."

This place smelled of death.

"I must leave soon."

"I thought you only just arrived."

"I'm on duty."

"Nobody wants to visit me. Even your sister does not come anymore."

"I don't have a sister. At least not one that I'm aware of."

His mother, Millicente, seemed to be reaching for a memory. She gazed for a long time through the window at the grey sky, as if she might find it there.

"Until next week then, Mother."

"Tell the girl I will be dining alone in my room this evening. That is all for now Hillaire. You are dismissed."

9

There was no light outside. She was confused, unsure how long she had slept. After Alphonse had made his calculations she had gone into her area of the room and fallen asleep. It was a conscious decision because she knew that sleep was an enhanced state of awareness and her questions were more likely to be answered, but if she had received direction in her dreams she had forgotten it.

Alphonse was out. He had helped her a lot, sharing his studio, listening to her ideas, and now providing her with clothes. They were friends, lovers even, up to a point. Beyond that was a wasteland, ringed by an ancient wall; the guards were all dead but the stones were un-breached. A fragment of tattered cloth hung down from a crenellation. Night was almost perpetual.

She felt excited. An epiphany was close.

She saw her reflection in the mirror, wearing the clothes he had given her. Alphonse did not own much. He had given her an old pair of trousers and a shirt. They were much too big, she had to belt the trousers with some string and roll them up to her calves. Luckily she had her own shoes, a pair she kept in the studio to paint in. She looked like a circus clown, or a cabaret singer. It wasn't bad.

The platform at Marcadet-Balagny was almost empty. Sophia leaned against the wall. She watched a heavyset man walk towards her, talking to himself. When he reached her he stopped and looked into her face.

"If I am half as bad as people think I am, I'm a bad man."

She had the sense that something important was underway. He paused for a moment as if waiting for a reply.

"Do you know who I am?"

He was not threatening, but he had the kind of personality which knew no bounds. He was right up against her, reaching into his coat and searching his pockets. Finally he produced a tattered identity card and thrust it under her nose. She had to wriggle herself away to focus.

The printed name on the card had been heavily crossed out, and above it was written 'Napoleon Bonaparte' in cursive script.

"I thought you died on St. Helena."

"I might as well have. Everyday I went to look down on the sea for a ship that would come and take me to Toulon. One day a ship arrived but I had to become someone else to slip past the Englishman. I was so successful that I've never been able to get back to who I was before. No one recognizes me now."

"Surely there are people in Paris who could help you."

"In Paris, memory is short. I have been forgotten."

"Friends?"

"Friendship is only a word."

Sophia sensed that she was losing him.

"What is it that you want?"

"What do I want?"

He tucked the card away and looked up and down the platform.

"I want something to eat… I had ambition once. Stupid people blamed it for all the wars I started. They didn't understand the nature of life, the tension between the future and the past. In the end it came down to destroy or be destroyed. I wanted to create a United States of Europe."

"Do you still want that?"

"No. I've had enough of war and politics. How can anyone with my girth still have ambition? But if I had succeeded I would have been the greatest man ever known."

"Could I ask you for advice?"

"About what?"

"If I was to tell you that there is a place, a kind of citadel, which I mean to take and restructure, to topple the monarchs and create a United States of the Mind, what would you say?"

She could hear the roar of the approaching train. He had to shout.

"Go to the Gare du Nord. Remember that a man is not great because he is lucky. He is lucky because he is great."

Napoleon disappeared within seconds as the train pulled away, both hands on his hat. Sophia was soothed by the metallic noises of the carriage on the track. They mumbled to her in an incomprehensible language, reciting a mechanical poem. She could not remember feeling so alive. The reflections in the windows portrayed the passengers in old age. A man who looked like a veteran walked through the carriage repeatedly saying: "Like it or not, I'm your lieutenant."

The door of number seventy-one was unlocked, as she had left it. She only locked it when she was present. There was nothing worth stealing except her. She found a pair of scissors and cut the string around her waist, allowing the trousers to glide past her hips and form a heap around her ankles. After a brief entanglement, she stepped out of them and went to bed. As she laid her head against the cold pillow, she fell asleep thinking of half a walnut. Its brain-like meat was packed into the wrinkled shell, just visible beyond the thin partition. She wondered which hemisphere was missing.

She explained her plan, if that is what it was, to the man she noticed sitting in the chair across from her bed. He had introduced himself to her as Sr. Lopez de Balboa. He was definitely a gentleman, erudite and eccentric with the bright eyes of the blind. His cheeks radiated good health. He knew much more of what she was talking about than she did.

They were discussing the significance of the modern railway station in the form of a nounal reduction. Connection, movement, power, organization, notice boards, timetables. Their words bounced back and forth, ping pong balls, which she would slam and he would spin. As her luck would have it, he knew more about the Central Station than any other living person, though he referred to it as *Casa de León.*

When he was a young man he had worked for the building firm which had won a contract for a major renovation there.

"It always needed to expand, but downwards."

It was a very beautiful building, simple in form, the colour of sunset. There were no windows or doors other than a decorative, non-functional door on one face. The interior was divided into different rooms, each one named for its function. The room in which Christianity was manufactured and maintained, for example, was known as *The Hall of the Preterists.* Everything was a hall. It might have been a joke among the architects, sarcastically referring to the cramped conditions. They had devised an ingenious way to fold space in on itself to make it all fit. After the work was completed the firm was forced into bankruptcy through some corporate sleight of hand, and the partners dispersed. Within a year every single person who had been involved in the project had died under mysterious circumstances. Sr. de Balboa escaped with his life but lost his sight. It had left him with an unremitting hatred of the *Casa de León.*

"How do you get in then, if there are no doors?"

"You don't. Those that are in are in. Everyone else is out."

The priest officers who kept the machine running spent their lives in the building. Either time was slower there, or the evolutionary process, stimulated by extreme isolation, had sped up, for the people inside were no longer exactly human. They gave birth to themselves before they died.

Outside, one had to contend with the Margrave's men—all of them brutal thugs, and with the Margrave himself, who was a ruthless sadist of abnormal intelligence.

"But I'll tell you a secret. There is a way in. We built it ourselves—the workmen who wanted to be architects. To get in, you crawl up the lion's asshole."

It was Sr. Balboa's opinion that she was going to need assistance. He would introduce her to some like-minded people, mechanics, anarchists and rakes.

They left immediately without shutting the door.

10

Sr. Lopez de Balboa led her to *La Barbe Russe* on Rue de Buci. He was sure-footed for someone who could not see. They walked between the tables on the street and through the interior to the back of the room. He instructed her to make the sign of the fork by curling her ring finger and holding it in place with her thumb while leaving the other three extended. This would guarantee them access to the back stairs without molestation. They turned left at the top and went into a small room. There were shelves against the walls containing restaurant supplies, and a table with half a dozen chairs strewn around it—a place where waiters could come for cigarette breaks. Three people were sitting and one was standing. Sr. de Balboa made the introductions.

The first person she met was the standing man, Hamish 'Grim' McCormick. He was red-headed with a thin, acned face, which seemed to be out of proportion to the rest of his body. During the war he had been a sapper in the Royal Engineers. After being demobbed in 1919 he had become an inveterate masturbator. A decade of overindulgence rendered the pastime of no further interest and he turned instead to the study of knots. For him the act of cutting a knot, as opposed to untying it, was a crime. He was an explosives expert and always carried concealed grenades, one in each armpit, supported by an elaborate harness of his own design, and a belt-load of them around his waist, which explained his odd proportion.

Sophia learned these details in several minutes of hoarse whispering from Rosa Schmidt, a German communist and the only other woman present.

She also discovered that the two brothers, Pedro and Raffael Gonzalez had been auto mechanics in Buenos Ares until they were accused of theft and dismissed. What had been stolen was not specified.

Rosa was chatty and domineering. She was from Hamburg and gave a vague explanation as to why she was in Paris, which in her own words "had to do with falling foul." She was a potent mixture of rigid political opinion and a libidinous sexuality. "I would kill to have more orifices than three," she confided in a stage whisper.

They were all united in their awareness of the Central Station, which each one of them called by a different name, and in their desire to bring it down, though they could not agree as to how that should be done.

Rosa favoured splitting it into regional councils and executing the current authorities, after a fair trial. Hamish thought the answer was annihilation, to be accomplished by scientifically placed charges beneath the structure. The Gonzalez brothers were more concerned with re-wiring. Sophia was uncertain, not having thought about such things but she tended towards the Gonzalez idea, for total destruction would preclude the transformation she had imagined, and where would it leave humanity? Rosa's idea of councils was too dogmatic and dull.

Lopez de Balboa did not engage in the conversation but sat in an armchair on the other side of the room, listening to them with a hint of amusement on his lips. He withdrew a small book from his pocket and held it for a while. It revealed itself, upon opening, to be not a book but a solander containing a metal snuff box. He took a hefty sniff, and seconds later emitted a loud sneeze which interrupted the conversation and they all stopped talking.

"Hearing you talk makes me think of the word 'Dreamtime'—you're planning a revolution in dreamtime. An intriguing idea but it has some problems—mostly semantic. What is dreamtime but the mistranslation of the word *alcheringa*? And even that is perhaps the wrong word—garbled, misunderstood, or willfully manipulated to fit a theory. Thoughts can be limiting. Anyway, time doesn't exist in dreams as far as I know."

Sophia was not sure exactly what he meant. She liked the sound of dreamtime, but she suspected that his whole outburst, including the monstrous sneeze was calculated to reaffirm his authority. It cast him in a different light, more patronising than friendly.

After that they resumed their discussion, though not with the same unselfconscious gusto as before. They couldn't reach a unanimous decision about what to do with the Central Station. Sophia had assumed that if she sided with Raffael and Pedro, the re-wiring idea would be chosen but the other two did not have the temperaments to honour a democratic vote unless it was to their liking. In the end they agreed to postpone the decision until they got there and took stock of the situation.

They were talking about where it was and how to reach it, when they heard three knocks on the floor, followed by four and then two. What little colour Pedro had in his face, drained away instantly.

"We have to go."

There was a frantic scramble as they leapt from their chairs. Sr. de Balboa stayed seated.

"Señor. Please come quickly."

"No. I'll only slow you down. Don't worry about me. I can talk my way out of this, besides, what are they going to do with an old blind man?"

Hamish was agitated.

"I'll show them. I'll detonate myself."

"No, no. That's not necessary. This way. Quickly."

Pedro seemed to be familiar with the place. He led them along the hallway, down another staircase into the kitchen, through a trapdoor in the floor, across the basement to a sticky side door, which needed forcing, and up into the street where they disappeared into the city as mist evaporates in the sunlight.

11

Far beneath the Gare du Nord was a subterranean river. Pedro knew the way. Perhaps Sr. de Balboa had told him. It took a long time to get down there in total darkness. Eventually we saw light. We had come to a dock where a paddle steamer was moored. Pedro led us straight on board. No one questioned us. There weren't any other passengers and the crew was nowhere to be seen. We were running from the watchers and we were all nervous. It was a relief when the engines started and the boat pulled away.

Our journey was claustrophobic and oppressive. It seemed that the tunnel we were passing through was barely larger than the boat. Occasionally it opened out but that was not much better.

There was an endless chthonic gloom around us, and the smell of damp and mould permeated everything. Sometimes the engines would go silent and we would drift for a while. Then our ears would be assaulted by dripping and gurgling sounds that lapped away at our optimism. It's hard to say how long we were down there. Ten days perhaps. There was nothing much to do but sleep. I had a fling with Rosa. She was intense, but then so was I.

After days in darkness we saw a glow ahead of us and the boat burst into the sunlight. It was agony but we all came out on deck to squint through our fingers. I hadn't seen the others for most of the trip and it was almost pleasant to meet Hamish again, looking like a woodlouse. Once I had become used to the light I gazed out over the side, enjoying my restored vision. There was dense vegetation on both banks stretching into the distance. I thought it must be the Amazon, or the Orinoco—one of those places I had only heard about.

Food was a problem. We had ransacked the galley and

found some biscuits and a few old tins. Now they were gone and we were beginning to starve. Even the exposure to light didn't prevent the return of listlessness. The crew were no help. They must have been there but we never saw them. There was an occasional noise which suggested their presence. The door up to the bridge was locked. I think they were ghosts.

Whoever they were, they docked the ship one day against an old makeshift quay, built from logs lashed with vines, slimy and rotten from the river. Then I think they must have left. They obviously scuttled the vessel first, because we noticed it was taking on water and beginning to list. We went ashore. There was a hut with nothing in it but two rusty machetes, which we took. Then we set off into the jungle. When we left, the bow had risen up out of the water at an unnatural angle.

The going was hard and slow. We were bitten incessantly by insects. Hookworms burrowed into our flesh and Pedro dug them out with the tip of his knife. Leeches attached themselves to us. The noise of birds and animals was unremitting, I hadn't noticed them so much on the boat. It was only my resolve that made it possible for me to continue. I had come this far, I couldn't succumb before I reached the Central Station. Hamish was surprisingly resilient. I think his inner conflicts were so great, that he barely noticed the hardship. I'd always had the feeling that he wanted to blow himself up. On the boat when we had emerged from the tunnel, he confided to me that he was plagued with a melody that ran through his mind incessantly. It even invaded his dreams. He told me it was a nursery rhyme. He must have been shell-shocked. Pedro and Raffael seemed like technicians, or engineers. They didn't have the kind of baroque imagination that I had. They were pragmatic. They met problems head on and dealt with them intelligently. Raffael was painfully quiet, Pedro was the dominant one and we naturally saw him as our leader, though he never told us what to do. I assumed he knew where he was going. It turned out he had no idea. I'm not sure why those two brothers wanted to go to the Central Station. I think it had something to do with changing the history of their country.

Rosa had been getting difficult even before we came ashore, complaining constantly. Now she was quickly unravelling. She kept falling back and sitting down, sometimes combatively speechless and at other times shouting out to us to abandon her, when we knew she meant the opposite. She was slowing us down, and in our situation we needed all the speed we could muster. It was a matter of life and death. But then one day, as she sat howling on the ground, refusing to move, she was bitten by a snake and died almost instantly.

The two brothers tended to her. Hamish and I were up ahead. They carried her off, further into the jungle, for an improvised burial. I doubt they would have been able to dig a grave with machetes. Pedro carried a canvas bag over his shoulder which contained a few tools and some sundries but I don't think they had a shovel.

Rosa's sudden death did not even seem real to me. She had such a strong personality and we had been so close. But exhaustion and hunger dulled my emotions. My sadness became resignation.

We followed the course of the river, as best we could, in the direction that it flowed. At night we took turns to take watch while the others tried to sleep. No one really slept because of the biting insects and the noises in the dark. On the first night Pedro pulled some meat out of his bag. He said he had scavenged it. Raffael wouldn't touch it. I managed to swallow a few mouthfuls. I knew what it was. Life had changed so drastically—from being a painter in Paris to eating the raw flesh of my lover. My previous existence seemed bland compared to this struggle for survival. It was surprising that among so much abundance we could find so little to eat. After that first and only act of cannibalism we subsisted on leaves and bark, and ants which we swallowed alive. We drank from the river.

Our rest stops became more frequent as our stamina ebbed. We didn't have much to say to each other and retreated into ourselves. Hamish began untying his bootlaces and re-tying them with a different knot each time. He had elegant fingers.

"See… A love knot."

I traced the two cords as they met, wrapping around each other, intertwining, penetrating. It was indeed a sensuous knot. As I watched him tying his other boot, delaying his deftness so I could follow what he did, I understood the significance of a knot, the knowledge required to tie it, the need for its invention—a maritime purpose perhaps—ships, exploration, trade, the meetings of people, the survival of life through the ages, the civilization which could so easily vanish, and I believed I understood now why Hamish would never cut a knot.

His boots were tied and it was time to move on again. Raffael was as taciturn as ever but Pedro had started muttering to himself. He kept talking about the absurdity of looking for a place that didn't exist. The strain was obviously getting to him. I had never had any doubts about finding the Central Station. The absurdity of the venture just seemed to indicate an increased likelihood of success. Absurdity is on a par with divinity in my opinion.

After hacking our way through dense brush for days, civilization reappeared. A swathe of land had been deliberately cleared. Stretched over it were coils of barbed wire and beyond them a red brick wall, probably four metres high. Our energy returned. Hamish was in his element.

"Have you got any wire cutters in that bag of yours?"

Pedro produced a pair that looked far too small for the job. Hamish took them with a shrug, and lying down on his stomach, set to work. He squeezed and cursed in pain. Eventually, with much effort, he was able to cut a hole big enough to pass through.

"There may be mines. Follow directly behind me at a distance."

We did as he said, and followed him as he painstakingly worked his way toward the wall, feeling the ground as he went, scouring it with his eyes and carefully probing for detonators. First Hamish, then Raffael, then me, and finally Pedro crawled in a line and reached the wall unscathed. I stood up gingerly and put my hands on the red bricks. Hamish and Raffael walked further along it, towards the river, looking for an opening. There was none. It was an impenetrable expanse of uniformity, perfectly laid and insurmountable. Pedro was just telling me that he thought we might be able to get over it by climbing up on each other to form a human ladder, when there was a massive explosion. Hamish and Raffael were killed immediately. Whether it was deliberate, or because one of them had stepped on a mine, I could not say. But Hamish must have done it. I had always suspected he would. We picked ourselves up; Pedro's cheeks were streamed with tears. A section of the wall had collapsed and I could see the Central Station, just as Sr. de Balboa had described it.

Well almost as he had described it, for on the side of the building was a colossus of a lion, which looked like it was made of bronze, and he hadn't mentioned it—except for its asshole.

"I know this is difficult but we have to go through."

Pedro showed no sign of moving. He seemed defeated.

"Is this worth the cost? Three lives? My own brother?"

The noise of the explosion was going to attract attention. The Margrave's men might already be on their way.

"If we don't move soon, we'll be done for, and the cost will be even higher."

A horse cantered by us as we crossed through the breach. It was riderless but that didn't allay my fears. It did tell me though, that we didn't have to worry about a minefield. I started to run; Pedro followed. When we reached the building, we skirted along the edge, towards the river and the lion.

"There's no way in."

The smooth stucco of the walls was a pale lemon, but the tone was varied, sometimes moving towards rose and orange. The building was separated from the sky by a grey parapet. When we got around to the side facing the lion, which was decorated to look like the front, I saw that the parapet arched up in a semicircle. Within the arch were two flat disks, and on top, a stone ball. Running down from the roof were two columns and between them was the door that was not a door. To the left of that was a window that was not a window.

"There is a way in. We just have to go up the lion's asshole."

I told him what Sr. de Balboa had said about the secret entrance. It was one thing to crawl up the asshole but first we had to reach it.

The lion was almost as tall as the building it guarded. It stood on a massive stone plinth, parallel to the Central Station and the river, looking outward into the jungle beyond. On either side of it was a line of manicured trees. Everything about the statue was improbable, from the size of the stone it stood on, to the prodigious casting. The asshole must have been a good fifteen metres above the ground. We would have been better off as circus performers. Pedro stood and stared upwards. He couldn't resist trying to solve a problem. After a few minutes he told me he had an idea. The lion had a long tail which angled out from the main structure and curved downwards. It might be reachable from one of the trees. He had a hank of rope. We could cut two lengths, which we could use to belt ourselves to the tail. With that support, we would be able to climb up. The whole plan was contingent on being able to get to the tail from the tree. Pedro shimmed up and confirmed it could be done. Such a climb would leave us exposed for a considerable time, so we decided to wait until dark and hid ourselves in the bushes near the wall by the river.

There had been no sign of the Margrave's men. I wondered why that was, if they were so fierce and efficient. As I began to doze I imagined that they had all lost their jobs in the Great Crash.

Pedro shook me awake. It was dark. He had already cut the rope and handed me my belt. It was hemp, stiff and hairy. He told me it was rated for more weight than both of us combined, so everything depended on a good knot. It made me think of Hamish. We scurried out to the tree in the moonlight. There were three moons, in different stages of fullness, and between them there was enough light for us to see what we were doing. We climbed the tree. Pedro went first. He had already tied his rope into a loop and threw it on to the tail, then he pulled himself up. It was strong enough to bear his weight, which had been a concern of ours. He supported himself while pushing the rope further up the tail and wriggled into it as he let it back down. Then he swung himself under the tail and began to climb, using his hands and feet, supported by the rope. I did the same. I had tied a reef knot, the only one I knew. I hoped it would hold.

The ascent was slow and painful. When we finally arrived at the perineum, we discovered a narrow shelf-like extrusion. We hung from the tail, the ropes across our chests and under the armpits, our feet upon the shelf. It was difficult to see as we were blinded by our own shadows.

"It doesn't have an asshole."

"It's a fucking statue, that's why."

I thought of what I had abandoned—a life of painting and people, of enjoyment and excitement, to hang suspended from a giant statue in the middle of nowhere, so close to my desire but denied satisfaction. It made me angry, and supported by the rope, I kicked at it.

There was a noticeable variation in tone when my feet hit different areas—from a dead sound to a more resonant one. I could also tell that the surface was flexing under my blows.

Pedro managed to reposition himself so that he could use his hands. He took his knife from his bag, which he had tied to his stomach for the climb, and scratched the surface. He said it was sheet metal, probably copper. He pierced it. The metal was not thick. Using his blade as a tin opener, he made a series of close holes until he could pry it open. We crawled in. There was a platform on the other side with a metal runged ladder leading down. Pedro put his knife away.

"You'd think that someone who went to the trouble of making a concealed entrance would have done a better job. It was too easy. As if they wanted us to find it."

We climbed down the ladder to the inside of the plinth and found a tunnel which obviously led to the building. All this we did in darkness, which by now we were used to.

We emerged through a hatch into the Central Station. It was illuminated. The floor was a grille of wrought iron, mildly ornate in a floral way, and something you might have expected to find in a pavilion at the Great Exhibition. We could look down through it to the floor below, and to the floor below that. It was as difficult to count the number of floors beneath us, as it was those above. These floors ran around the perimeter, making the interior walls look like a building within a building. There were doors, about three metres apart, and a staircase in each exterior corner. Everything was identical. Going up seemed a better prospect than going down, so we climbed a few flights, reading the nameplates on the doors we passed.

The Hall of Mamadilo, *The Hall of Janus*. Just as Sr. de Balboa had said, everything was the hall of something. I was looking for *The Hall of the Preterists*, partly because it had stuck in my mind since our conversation, and also because I instinctively felt that this was the area where my sabotage would most benefit humanity. It was personal too. I've never been able to stomach religion of any kind.

There wasn't any discernible order to the names on the doors and I soon noticed that you had only one chance to read them. If you turned your head away and then looked back again, the names were changed or the letters jumbled.

The place was so big, and there was so much choice, that it was obvious we would not be able to make the sweeping changes I had imagined. A faint whirring sound came from behind the closed doors, otherwise there was complete silence.

We had climbed five flights when *The Hall of the Preterists* caught my eye. I looked again. It was *The Hall of the Mountain Kings*, but I knew I was not mistaken.

"Let's go in here."

I tried the door handle. It turned, and we stepped inside. The room was small and rectangular. The floor was cement, painted light grey. The walls were the same colour. To the left of the door was an open cabinet recessed into the wall, from floor to ceiling. It was packed with thousands of coloured wires, so densely tangled I couldn't take my eyes from them. Some were harnessed together in bundles but most of them formed a huge amorphous mass which spilled into the room. There was a similar cabinet in the adjacent wall and next to that there was some kind of control panel with five circular gauges and a bank of switches. Below that, behind a glass door, were copper pipes with hoses attached, and a coil of copper tubing. There was also a box which Pedro said was a relay.

The idea we had talked about, of rewiring the Central Station, no longer seemed possible. We could spend months in this room alone, so we decided to cut as many wires as we could and then reconnect the different ends. We had no idea what we were doing, or how effective it would be.

We had to move quickly, there were more rooms to visit and Pedro wanted to find *The Hall of Solis*. He took the wire cutters from his bag and started to cut, stripping away the insulation as he went. I twisted the ends together, making sure to join only different coloured wires.

After making about twenty connections it was time to go. I opened the door a crack and listened, then I stuck my head out. There was no sign of patrolling priest officers, so we walked out into the corridor, quietly shutting the door behind us.

I had just stepped onto the staircase, leading up to the next level, when Pedro suddenly lurched forward. I turned in surprise. There was a man in uniform on his back, snarling and tearing into his neck. Behind them was another man, narrow faced with a thin moustache, dressed expensively. He looked familiar. He stood for a few minutes, fascinated by the attack. Then he finally stepped forward.

"That's enough. Stand down."

The attacker reluctantly raised himself. He was more hominid than human, with short pointed ears and a simian face, which was bloodied from the gorging. Pedro lay still. I saw that the back of his neck had been eaten away.

Fingers gripped my arm and I was pushed against the wall, my hands pulled behind my back. I heard the snap and felt the cuffs close on my wrists, then a soft voice in my ear.

"Got you."

This is how I came to this place.

12

Dr. Lavoisier took his fingers from the Remington and sat back in his chair, swinging a foot on to the desk. He picked up the handwritten pages he was transcribing and started to read them again. He had given Sophia a pencil and paper and asked her to record her thoughts as to why she was in hospital. It was a fascinating account and far exceeded his expectations. He ran the fingers of his free hand over the filigree designs that bordered the green leather on his desktop. His skill with the Remington was minimal. It was going to take a long time to type out this account. He was in no hurry though, and his frequent pauses gave him time to think.

His first impression was that it read like an account of a dream with an impressive degree of recall. There was some emotion expressed but it had a flatness in its connection to events. Two men are blown to pieces but the focus is on a strange building seen through a broken wall. There were other oneiric indicators such as the names on the doors, which changed each time they were looked at.

Dr. Lavoisier had been visiting Sophia daily since she had been admitted to Salpêtrière. She slipped in and out of lucidity. Sometimes he was able to hold a relatively normal conversation with her, as when he had asked her to write down her thoughts. At other times she would remain motionless and say nothing, or talk apparent nonsense. She seemed to think he was a fellow prisoner. Ironically she had a point. He was looking forward to the day when he could leave this hospital and practice privately. Though he was generally respected he felt hemmed in by the politics. His approach to work, which he regarded as informed intuition, often caused tension with the hospital authorities and other staff members, who were more rigid in their opinions.

Sophia was confined to her own room, on the insistence of

the police, who had brought her in, and with the connivance of Dr. Roget. They were convinced that she posed a risk and was possibly associated with a dangerous group of anarchists. It seemed ridiculous to him, but there was nothing he could do about it. They had discovered her in an operations room in the Gare du Nord, not open to the public. As far as he knew, she had been found alone and had not caused much damage. He was more concerned with diagnosis and treatment, than with punishment.

Her provenance was also an interesting story. In a moment of clarity she had told him she was an orphan and had been raised by nuns at the abbey in Collombey-Muraz, Switzerland. Just a few days previously, her parents had visited. He'd had a private discussion with them and learned that she had grown up in Paris, an only child in a comfortable home. Her father was a chemist. They had tried to discourage her from becoming an artist but she had fled to Zurich in 1916, when still just a teenager, and had become involved with the Dadaists. Her parents were torn about it, as they felt that her stay in Switzerland had kept her safe from the war but had also set her on the path which ultimately led to this institution. The only point on which both these differing accounts agreed was Switzerland.

Dr. Lavoisier got up from his desk. He bent over to unlace his shoes and removed them. Then he pulled a box from a shelf and spilled its contents on to the carpet. He knelt in front of a mound of wooden blocks. Before long he was building a structure and pulling away pieces to create small caves which reminded him of the way the Romans had quarried stone in Les Beaux, leaving negative space in the mountainside.

He tried to spend at least half an hour every day at this pastime, which he called *Ludic Disengagement*. Most of his colleagues would probably not understand, but it had a very definite purpose. He recognized the importance of play in the development of the imagination. It was also a relaxing way to put aside his adult concerns and build something just for pleasure. He often found that it helped him find solutions to problems. When he had cleared up the blocks, he jotted down some notes with his pen.

What illness would manifest itself with the inability to differentiate between dream and waking state?

Is this an illness, or something else?

Have I seen anything similar?

What does the dream describe?

Why is her past falsified?

Dr. Roget had quickly reached the diagnosis of schizophrenia but Lavoisier wasn't so sure. Roget was prone to over-confidence. There was something unusual about Sophia, which he could not identify. He was interested in artists, often more than the works they created.

He was going to enjoy teasing information out of this text. Pen in hand, he waited.

The first thing that struck him was the number five.

There were five people in the boat, three men and two women. The number five—odd and prime. Being an odd number, it might suggest a lack of equilibrium—three on one side, two on the other. Then there was the reference to the body. Five digits on a hand or foot. Thinking of the body brought to mind a pentagram—the body with feet apart and arms outstretched, head on top—a five pointed star. Each point representing a different character in her narrative.

If the five characters could be considered different aspects of herself, then the two brothers might represent the practical, problem-solving personae who navigate day to day existence. The emotionally wounded soldier, Hamish, is a destructive element. A symbol of pain and anger. The love knot he ties with his laces, suggests a sexual attraction to the annihilation he represents, tangled like the forest through which they pass. Thanatos. It is interesting that she acknowledges that this man is damaged. It could be that he is also symbolic of the war. Such a traumatic event would be ingrained in the psyche of every European. The barbed wire is another such image. She regards these aspects of herself as male. That is unsurprising given the roles ascribed to the different sexes by society at large. The German communist Rosa Schmidt is her libido. Why German and why a communist? Is it because, as a modern artist she is pushing the socio-sexual boundaries? Then Germany as a recent foe and communism as a nascent threat to the establishment would be fitting. The colour red, associated with communism, was the colour of blood and might also be equated with sexuality, or menstruation. Could it be that simple?

The uppermost point of the star would be the synthesis of these characters and represent the self which exists in the external world. The Ego. She displays a combination of determination and passivity. She sees herself as being acted upon but as the story progresses she becomes less passive and eventually is the only one to survive. This might suggest a psychic growth, the path from initiate to initiated. The boat, the tunnels, the subterranean river, the bursting out of darkness into light, all seem self-evident. A passage from the subconscious land of the dead in a vessel floating on a Styx-like continuum, through the birth canal, and born into a different state of existence. There is a ritual significance to this—a symbolic death and rebirth, quite common among the world's myths and religions. The present but invisible, ghostly crew might represent the autonomous vital functions of the body.

That element of ritual is also corroborated by the deliberate sinking of the vessel. The scuttling occurs only after the passengers have disembarked, which suggests a necessary abandonment of the self, if the desired goal is to be achieved. There is no return.

The travellers make their way through the jungle, the primeval wilderness outside of consciousness, impenetrable and hostile. This is the way to the oddly named Central Station, which sounds more American than French. The choice of this name is interesting, seeing as she was apprehended in the Gare du Nord. What is the significance of a train station?

Death stalks them. First the libido perishes, unsurprisingly bitten by the phallic snake, creature of the underworld and possessor of sexual knowledge. The ensuing cannibalism represents taking the life force of the vanquished. She is, by extension, eating herself. In the act of eating, survival and death are inseparable. All of this underscores the metaphor of ritual.

The silent partner of practicality and the destructive soldier are the next to die, in a violent explosion, which she knows will happen. Their demise allows the wall to be breached and reveals the Central Station.

What of the building with no external doors or windows? You can neither enter nor leave. The static point at the centre of chaos. The fulcrum. She refers to it as civilization. She describes it in a way that brings to mind a Spanish colonial mansion. Her earlier references to the Amazon and to the mysterious Sr. de Balboa, suggest one of those legendary lost cities of South America, which the conquistadors believed in so literally. A place of great riches and hidden knowledge.

There is a secret way in—up the lion's posterior. Mentioned frequently. A metaphor of sodomy, with underlying humour in the description.

Three animals of significance are mentioned in the account—the serpent, the horse and the lion.

A riderless horse suggests an abrogation of control. But whose control? Is it Sophia's, in an initiatory capacity, or is it the Margrave's? The Margrave seems to be some sort of Teutonic authority figure, and might hark back, in a general sense, to the recent European cataclysm. She exhibits a paranoid fear of authority. The 'watchers' she mentions are also an example of it.

The lion, another symbol of power and nobility, is in this case a statue—a symbol of a symbol. It is an interesting abstraction and perhaps denotes the act of consciousness observing itself. Is it coincidence that the only way into the sealed building is through the sentinel who guards it? Or could it be a Trojan Horse?

The inside of the building has a multitude of doors. Possibilities and points of transition are potentially infinite. The names on the doors are obscure, and keep changing. There is an irony that written names, which are intended to clarify, only obfuscate. That is common enough in dreams.

Her desired destination is *The Hall of the Preterists*. She has a contempt for the Christian Church, which is widespread among contemporary artists. The use of the word 'Preterists' denotes an interest or belief in the past, or theologically with eschatology. How does this relate to the falsification of her own past?

They pass by *The Hall of Mamadilo*—female African water spirit, a seductress who abducts people from rivers, and *The Hall of Janus*—the two-headed Roman god of the doorway and transition. Her chosen door changes its name to *The Hall of the Mountain Kings*—the music of Grieg for Ibsen's play *Peer Gynt*—a story of men and trolls that might describe individual isolation in society. In old age Peer Gynt meets a man on a boat who wants to examine his corpse to determine the origin of dreams.

The origin of dreams seems to be the purpose of the Central Station. The building has three general areas—the outside, the inside, and the inside of the inside. An interesting spatial concept. Each area has a different architectural style. They range from South American Spanish colonialism, through 19th Century industrial, to the present day and maybe beyond. Her sabotage is to change the wiring. Is not Art the making of new connections between existing ideas?

Pedro is killed by the half-human 'priest officer'. This being is a melding of religious and secular authority in her paranoid fantasies, therefore quite naturally expressed as man-ape. Another example of the Eating/Death theme. More interesting is the well dressed man who places her in handcuffs. She has completed an arduous quest successfully. She has divested herself of her worldly components, unified herself in an alchemical way, integrated herself. Then she is suddenly imprisoned. Could this be an interstitial point between two realities, the moment of waking from a dream? In that case was the man who cuffed her in the Central Station the actual police officer who arrested her in the Gare du Nord?

It was probably lunchtime. He could smell the hospital food wafting down the corridor and seeping through the crack beneath his door. He stopped writing and put down his pen. This was not so much an analysis as a free association of thoughts. It was a cursory preparation that would help him find a way to treat Sophia. A more detailed and carefully considered analysis of her case would follow but already it strengthened his opinion that this account was not the dream of an insane person. The moments of awareness and humour reinforced that. It was as if she inhabited a different reality but the internal logic was sound.

Sophia may have been immersed in madness but she had not been consumed by it. Everyone lived in their own reality. It was just a matter of degree. She could come out. It just remained for him to discover the cause of her psychosis, and in that respect he was no further along than when he had started. But Dr. Roget was wrong.

13

"No. I'm not a ghost."

Alphonse realised that his face must be expressing the surprise he felt at seeing someone unexpected. He had been standing at a shop window looking at his reflection when he became aware of another person behind him, also looking. He spun around.

"Jean Claude, you survived the fire."

"Yes. Either that, or I raised myself from the dead. But don't turn around."

Alphonse looked back to the window.

He had not seen Devereux for years, and now he was speaking to his reflection. If the circumstances had been different, he would have found it amusing.

"What happened?"

"There's no time to talk. You are in danger. Move away."

"I don't see any danger."

"That's why I'm telling you. Go now."

"But..."

Devereux had already left. Alphonse watched him turn the corner in his big coat, with his hat pulled down. The day had a different slant now.

He did not feel in any particular danger. Beyond giving away trivial details about his friends, he was an informer who had never really informed. He had done his best to stall. He had never been interested in infiltrating the surrealist secret society and always avoided any association with art movements, even if they courted him. Ferdinand must have some other purpose for him, or he would have dispensed with him years ago. All he wanted was to be left alone. Now he felt a tightening of the knot.

If it wasn't for Ferdinand's interference, he would be quite content. Instead his life was leaking, drip by drip. He was partially to blame. He could have refused outright and faced the consequences. Maybe he lacked courage, but he could never engage in anything that didn't interest him. Ferdinand's threats didn't interest him, there was always something else to think about. The longer it had gone on, the deeper he had been immersed. That was the nature of lies. He had decided to tell Sophia but she had disappeared and he had just missed his opportunity with Devereux.

Vivian had invited him to attend a concert at the Salle Pleyel. She was bringing along a new friend she wanted him to meet. They were going to see Maurice Ravel conducting the Parisian première of one of his own works—the *Piano Concerto in D Major For The Left Hand.* The pianist had lost his right arm. He looked at his watch. He had eleven minutes. He was going to arrive on time. Vivian would be late.

The evening stroll through the streets lifted his mood. There was just enough purpose to it, but not too much. He was able to enjoy the differences of light and shadow, and the unknown people he passed. A cloying anxiety about Sophia had been haunting him all day. He wondered where she was, and had a bad feeling about it.

He was pacing outside the concert hall when a taxi pulled up and Vivian got out with her friend, the same man he had seen her with at the Select.

"Alphonse darling, how are you? This is the man I told you about, Dr. Étienne Lavoisier."

They shook hands.

"We'd better get in before they close the doors."

Vivian sat between them. Alphonse looked across her to the doctor. He seemed to be in his mid-fifties. Clean-shaven, bushy eyebrows. Maurice Ravel had taken the podium. Alphonse was glad to be spared conversation. He was enjoying the sound of the orchestra tuning their instruments. He could listen to a whole concert of this, and there would be no need for a composer. Each instrument had its own intention, but taken as a whole it was an undulating bed of sound without any conscious organization. There was applause when the wounded pianist took the stage. He had apparently commissioned this work. Ravel tapped his baton and Alphonse closed his eyes.

A few seconds passed between the moment when the conductor engaged the orchestra and the first note was played. It was the tense silence of expectation. Then the double-basses and bassoons began to rise from nowhere, gently ominous, and gain in volume until they were joined by the horns.

He tried to be absorbed by the sound but it was impossible. Thoughts constantly distracted him. The music grew into a menacing, angular cacophony. He was reminded of the war. The crescendo ended in a burst of tympani and the orchestra fell silent again.

He opened his eyes. This was the long delayed moment when the piano would start. He wanted to see how a man would play with just one hand. Ravel stood completely still as the left hand rapidly hammered out clusters of notes. The pianist was Paul Wittgenstein, the philosopher's brother. Alphonse shut his eyes again. It sounded like two hands.

Vivian sat between her lovers. She glanced at Alphonse, his eyes were closed and she looked at his face. It was patrician in its delicate sculpture, but with no hint of entitlement. Those features and their accompanying intellect were what had attracted her to him. But he could be exasperating. He was quiet but not shy. He took no pleasure in dancing. He was private to the point of being secretive. His ideas made her own feel irrelevant. The concerns of most people—money, security, relationships, possessions—didn't interest him. He was a living negation.

She liked to paint and she was good at it. Alphonse thought so. She kept a studio in Paris. It was a change of pace from the diplomatic life. Somewhere to paint and have love affairs, where she could be herself. She was happy with her marriage and would never leave it, but she had always inclined towards polyandry. Why couldn't she love more than one man? It wasn't an option in the Foreign Service, at least not openly. She didn't want scandal to damage her husband's career. He would be First Secretary one day, and then Ambassador perhaps. They led a very social and comfortable life, full of interesting people. They had an unspoken agreement. Charles would never visit or talk about her studio and, aside from the time she took for herself, she would support him and be the charming diplomat's wife.

Vivian had been introduced to Étienne by a friend. She had seen him first as a client, in the small private practice he was developing. It was not that she was ill or unhappy. The masking of her nature for the sake of social conformity caused certain tensions, but her main reason for their weekly sessions was her desire to learn about herself. She wanted to know how she fit into the modern science of psychology. It was a luxury she could afford.

He had listened without judgement as she described her sexuality and artistic endeavours. One day she had invited him to her studio. Things were different after that. Étienne had spent the last twenty-four years in a loveless marriage.

As she sat between them, she wondered if she had done the right thing bringing these two men together. A vague idea that they might benefit each other had made her do it. She hoped there would not be problems.

They were standing outside on the Rue du Faubourg Saint-Honoré. It was cold. Vivian wanted to go to the Dôme Café for drinks. Alphonse insisted on walking. It would take about an hour to get to Montmartre, enough time to digest the music and develop a thirst.

"What did you think of it?"

"Sinister and austere."

"So you liked it then."

"I did."

They turned on to Avenue Victor Emmanuel, and then on to the Champs Elysées, coats tightly clasped, their backs to the big monument. Étienne wondered if Alphonse knew Sophia. It was possible, considering they were both Parisian artists. He was still searching for the cause of her hallucinations but a sense of professional candour prevented him from asking.

It was hard to draw Alphonse into conversation. He seemed more of a depressive than the exotic figure Vivian had conjured in her description. Perhaps it was his reaction to their triangular relationship.

"Were you in the army?"

"Yes. You?"

"I was an army doctor during the war."

"A surgeon in the field?"

"No. I started my career as an ophthalmologist but in the war I was assigned to psychological cases. Tragically fortunate I suppose, because that became my area of expertise."

"So you've been standing on the edge of reality ever since, like most of us."

He could see what Vivian had been talking about. Alphonse had a way of emphasizing the unexpected in the obvious. He turned things upside down succinctly and no doubt enjoyed it. He was cutting but not condescending.

Vivian would have preferred to take a taxi. She walked between them, garnering what warmth she could from their bodies, and listening to what they had to say to each other. Étienne wanted to make a detour and visit the church of Saint-Germain-des-Prés.

"I like looking at churches, especially old ones. Ideas represented as solid objects. This one is almost fifteen hundred years old."

"All buildings are ideas."

"You are an atheist I suspect."

"I don't think that much about religion or atheism."

"Not thinking about them doesn't make them go away."

"Maybe not, but are they...? Look at that!"

Alphonse had stopped walking and was looking at something on the pavement.

"What? Where?"

"Over there. In the shadow by the wall. It's a cabbage."

Etienne and Vivian were peering into the darkness, trying to follow his pointing finger.

"I don't see it."

"You don't? Really? Well that's because it isn't there."

They straightened themselves with smiles.

"You see what I mean? Your attention is drawn to something and you can't prevent yourself from thinking about it, even though it's not there. That's how I feel about religion and atheism."

They never made the detour, Étienne was out-voted. The Dôme was welcoming, with its convivial hubbub and clusters of warm lights. They sat at a table with banquettes. After several glasses of wine, Étienne felt relaxed enough to talk about what was on his mind. He did not allude to Sophia directly but mused hypothetically about a dream state that could not be differentiated from reality.

Alphonse did not recognize that as a problem, for if one stripped away the elements of life which were taken for granted, what was left but a dream? He expounded on his theory that reality was no more than the intersecting areas of a metaphorical Venn diagram.

"You have a point, philosophically at least but in a psychiatric ward it's a different story."

He had the impression that Alphonse was full of longing, but his object of desire was forever pushed further away by the act of reaching for it. His dispassionate approach to life was compensation for perpetual disappointment. It could be that he was just describing himself—the doctor who escapes his own complications by examining those of others.

Vivian wanted more details about the dream.

"I have a patient who thinks Salpêtrière is a prison and who arrived there after a long journey on an underground river, through an Amazonian jungle, with sex, death and cannibalism along the way. It was a quest. When she reached her goal she was arrested by the police and brought to the hospital. That's where there is a strange confluence of realities, and both states seem to overlap. I've never seen anything quite like it."

Alphonse put down his glass.

"Is this patient of yours an artist?"

"Yes. The interesting thing is the purpose of the journey. She described it very clearly, even by name..."

Their waiter arrived with their food. Alphonse was presented with a plate of sausages and mashed potatoes. Vivian dipped her fork into her salad. She had been feeling awkward since they'd arrived. She had sat down first and Alphonse had slid in beside her, Étienne opposite. It seemed to upset the balance of the evening. She would have preferred her own chair. The men did not seem to mind. She put down her fork.

"I've read that some indigenous Amazonian tribes don't make any differentiation between the physical world and the spiritual one."

"That's the shadow projected by their animistic beliefs. More interesting than our own. There's usually some intoxicant involved."

Alphonse was tipsy from his wine.

Despite his lack of interest in religion, he found animism quite appealing. It might just be anthropomorphism, but it was possible that everything, including inanimate objects, had a facet of consciousness. He could imagine an urban variation where each building, its gutters and gargoyles and the stones with which it was built, all had independent lives of their own. He might walk along Rue Notre Dame des Champs one day and be seduced by an amorous doorway. Maybe he really was in danger.

The conversation had moved on to politics when Alphonse rejoined it. Vivian was privy to information from the embassy but she felt more aligned to the world of artists than diplomats. The consensus among Charles and his friends was that the economic and political situation would almost certainly lead to another war. Reason was being replaced by will and truth by myth. It could not end well.

"Politicians either aspire to greatness or think they have already achieved it. It's a fatal error. Posterity will decide on them, with all the gravitas of a slut bestowing her favours."

Alphonse was getting on her nerves. It wasn't so much his sweeping statements, as his apparent lack of awareness of their inherent bias. Coming from someone who regarded himself as free from bourgeois baggage, it was particularly grating.

While the two men were discussing politics, Vivian had been quietly slipping money into Alphonse's pocket. He was perpetually broke but always offered to pay whenever they were out together. This time he would be able to. It was a way for her to alleviate her irritation with him.

As they parted, outside the cafe, Étienne gave Alphonse his card.

"Thank you for dinner. Please feel free to visit me. We can talk more."

"I will, thank you." Alphonse began to walk away. He stopped and turned.

"Does the Central Station mean anything to you?"

"It does."

"I thought so."

14

Dr. Roget walked along the corridor to Sophia's room. Lavoisier had run out of time as far as he was concerned. Talking with her had not proved effective. She seemed unable to understand the simplest of sentences, let alone respond intelligibly. A more aggressive treatment was needed.

The previous night he had looked in on her, with Inspector Labeau. The Inspector had become a frequent and unwelcome visitor at the hospital. He took an unusual interest in this patient, which crossed professional bounds. Dr. Roget was not in a position to deny him, due to a financial transgression of some years past. The Inspector had been quick to mention it. The fact that this polite but unpleasant man seemed to know all about him, made him uneasy.

He had made Labeau stand outside the door, as he wanted time alone with the patient, and also to make it clear who was in charge. Sophia was incoherent, and seemed to think he was a Spaniard, by the name of Lopez de Balboa, come to rescue her. Nothing he said could dissuade her from her delusions. When he brought the Inspector into the room, she suddenly became agitated, screaming and sobbing that he was the Doge and had betrayed her. Several times she referred to the policeman as the Margrave, and then she clammed up, refusing to speak further, her body tense and immobile. He had known then that more drastic measures were required, and had decided on his course of action. It was a good thing that Lavoisier was off duty for a few days, and not there to disagree with him.

Now, as he entered, Sophia was acting violently and had to be restrained. Three nurses were trying to truss her up in a straitjacket. One of them received a split lip.

They frogmarched her along the corridor to room 202. He followed them. To witness such animal fear, caused him sorrow and contempt in equal measure. It was an emotionally draining experience. He kept a level head by telling himself that he sought only to help, and not to punish.

He stood by, hypodermic in hand, as the nurses removed the straightjacket and pushed her down into the chair. They secured her wrists and ankles with straps and buckled her head into the leather restraining helmet. Dr. Roget stepped forward and squeezed the air bubbles from his syringe. The intravenous shot of curare quickly put an end to her struggles. He waited for the drug to take full effect. Soon, only her eyes continued to fight him. She was almost ready.

Her heart was about to burst. She was being suffocated by a great weight pressing down on her. She was panicking but only her mind flailed. Her body was paralysed. The Doge had done something to take away her limbs. Only her head remained.

Gradually, and with much mental effort, she was able to calm herself. An unbearably bright light was shining directly into her face. Even light was an instrument of violation in this place. The Doge leaned over her and peered into her eyes. She stared back into his.

"So your blindness was a lie."

"What do you mean? I'm not blind. I've….."

Her sudden accusation caught him off guard. He had to retain his professional composure and not allow himself to get emotionally engaged. He turned to the small trolley by the wall and took another syringe from the tray.

"Nurse, where is the Metrazol?"

"It should be there, Doctor."

"It should be there, but it isn't. Find me some, please."

The nurse went to the trolley and quickly found what he had been looking for. He took it from her without thanks. This business had been fraying his patience. He wished he could turn back the clock to the time before Miss Villeneuve had arrived at Salpêtrière. She had brought with her a chaos that was upsetting his equilibrium. It had raised spectres from his past, and it exacerbated his already fraught relationship with Lavoisier. It would be a good thing for everybody if Lavoisier got his wish and went into private practice full time. Life would be simpler. The fact was, he did not like Sophia Villeneuve but he knew he should not let his personal feelings interfere with his work. He had to be careful.

Dr. Roget turned towards Sophia, his white coat rustling. No more dawdling. It was time to commence the treatment.

"Who are you?"

Again, her question unnerved him. He had a feeling of doubt that he quickly brushed off.

"Come now, Miss Villeneuve, you know me. I am your doctor and I am treating you for your illness."

Sophia watched with rapidly increasing terror as the Doge came towards her. He was holding his syringe in such a way as to make it less visible, but she could see it. He was going to poison her and there was nothing she could do about it.

"*Salaud*!"

The Doge was now standing over her, peering down. "If you want to talk, then talk, but don't insult me. There is no point. You are wasting your time."

His hand was probing her arm. He was looking for a vein.

"You led us on just so that you could persecute us for the act you suggested yourself. You have lied, betrayed and murdered."

"Who have I betrayed? You were just too credulous, that's all, and too eager to believe what you wanted to. I just made use of that, as is my prerogative."

"But you hatched a plot only to catch the plotters, who were innocent before they met you."

"Don't be surprised. There is nothing new in that. People in power have been doing it for centuries. Fights and battles can be costly and their outcomes uncertain, so if you wish to neutralize your opposition you are better off joining it than fighting it. If you can't find an enemy, then create one. If I find out that you want to overthrow me, I will help you in that venture, and always have the upper hand because I'll always know more than you do. Your recent experience is a case-in-point."

He leaned over her face.

"You know, the *Casa de León* is a curious system, both open and closed simultaneously. It has to be that way in order to have fluidity and longevity. It is a system that requires constant maintenance and modernization. We let certain people in to make the changes we need. You were one such person. Perfectly suited for the job, I might add. Of course when the work is done, the knowledge must be lost. And so it is time now for your injection. You will see everything at once and will not be able to make sense of it. You will no longer pose a threat."

He was still having trouble finding a suitable vein.

"Ah. There we are."

His thumb depressed the plunger.

"And you wonder who I am. You see, the beautiful thing about me is that I don't exist."

She felt the strange pressure of the fluid as it entered her vein.

Sophia fell silent. Dr. Roget raised one of her eyelids with his thumb. Her eye was moving rapidly. He went over to the trolley and dropped the syringe into a stainless steel dish. Then he smoothed his jacket.

This was a new treatment, and not without risk. Results had been generally positive so far and he expected an improvement in Sophia. He would administer the second injection in six days. He hoped that next time there would not be as much raving. Though he was used to dealing with delusional patients, it was getting more difficult to remain unaffected. It was a stressful treatment for patient and doctor alike.

15

She is conscious of the large spaces between things as an ant scaling a mountain of sugar, where each crystal is a separate rock that needs to be probed and explored. The ascent is made through digression.

At the top of the mountain is a forest. Silver birch, oak and hawthorn. Bent over among the trees, druids gather wild herbs and stuff them into woollen bags. They will take them down and process them in ways that are doomed to be forgotten. Each one of these druids has studied for at least twenty years but all their knowledge will be lost as they do not write it down. They know how to write but prefer to transmit orally, and yet they refuse to say anything. She can hear the sea rolling up on to the shore and retreating. Very close, though impossible to reach, as she can find no evidence of it other than its sound. Beyond the herb gatherers is a bower, fashioned from bent saplings, woven with twigs and leaves and red flowers. It has been built by a large bird, which watches her from a tussock.

She is drawn towards the bower by the flowers that adorn it. Inside, leaves are strewn on the ground, deep and moist. There is a strong smell of decay. This odour is complex. It appears at first to be organic—the rotting of vegetable matter becoming soil. But in the humus there are other smells. She is reminded of urban slums. Crumbling cement eroded by water, burnt wood, urine and putrefied flesh, cities inseparable from meat. And then lavender, jellyfish, socks. The smell of dog shit.

The gentle sound of breaking twigs outside takes her attention away from these smells. A bird stands in the open doorway, a silhouette against blinding light.

"What do you think?"

"About what?"

"This palace I built."

When she doesn't reply, the bird continues.

"I'd say it was a stroke of genius. My best yet. I call this one Neuschwanstein. I've built quite a few. I build in the name of love."

The bird awaits an answer, his head slightly askance, looking at her through one beady eye. She can make out that he is a handsome bird, solid, with black feathers, slightly glossy and tinted with the blue of mountains in the evening. He hops on to his other leg.

"I am a connoisseur of love, an adept you might say. Would you like to see my… ?"

"No, I would not. Thank you."

There is an awkward pause. Then he seems to un-ruffle his feathers and relax.

"Well, that's probably for the best. It's a relief really. I feel I can talk to you candidly. There's a lot of pressure on me, a lot of expectation. But the truth is… I prefer my own kind, if you know what I mean. You're not a Sapphist are you?"

"Can you fly?"

"Fly? Of course, I'm a bird."

"There are such things as flightless birds."

"Yes. Those that would be mammals."

With a sudden and surprisingly powerful flap of wings, and a cascading sound like the running of a stick along a fence, he lifts himself from the ground. He quickly gains altitude in sweeping circles, finds a thermal and soars even higher. He is about a hundred years away, when he breaks through the membrane of the sky. Water pours down through the hole he has made. At that moment of piercing, the sky reveals itself for what it is—an ocean viewed from just below the surface.

Once breached, the ocean sky begins to give up its secrets. The gushing water widens the hole until a geyser shoots downwards, bringing with it an assortment of celestial junk. An army of statues falls to the ground. Each one has a limb, raised in a calcified salute, that snaps off the body on impact. Gargoyles follow suit, headrests, religious paraphernalia, oranges, reams of paper, cutlery and shoes. Everything that falls widens the hole, which allows more objects through, and the reaction continues at an exponentially increasing rate until soon there is no hole at all. It is a coupling of earth and sky. All light is extinguished.

16

After two days off work, Dr. Lavoisier walked through the Mazarin entrance at Salpêtrière. He felt optimistic as he looked through the familiar archway to the one beyond, a sight that had always pleased him. He didn't know exactly what he was going to do, but he had a direction and his confidence for a diagnosis had increased. But when he reached his office, he discovered that Roget had made an irresponsible decision without consulting him. It must have happened on the night he had gone to the Salle Pleyel.

Sophia was now paying for Roget's headstrong approach to medicine. She was in a cataleptic state, mute and unresponsive. She displayed no sign of sensation when he gently pricked her forearm with a needle, no knee jerk from his rubber mallet. She lay on a bed, beneath a blanket. It was a state far worse than when she had arrived.

Roget was the type of person who became a doctor for status and money, not because of a natural vocation. Patients took second place to his own aspirations. It was a crime really, if you considered the Hippocratic oath. He might be a good technician, but his capacity for empathy was not developed enough to make him a good doctor.

The morning after the Ravel concert, Dr. Lavoisier had woken up late. His wife was away for the week, visiting her parents. It was something she did from time to time, and from which he usually abstained. He enjoyed having time to himself. It was a luxurious feeling like brushing against velvet. He took a moment to think about it as he ate his breakfast.

Afterwards he went into his study, a room he also used for his private practice. This was his personal domain. It was tidy, but not fastidiously so. He saw it as a reflection of his mind.

He let his eyes drift across the bookshelf. A work by Henri

Bergson caught his attention—*Creative Evolution*. He pulled it out and set it on the floor. A philosophy that valued intuition over rationalism in the comprehension of reality or, duration as he called it, seemed like a good way to start the day. It was a philosophy of mobility and becoming.

He took his second box of building blocks—the other one lived permanently in his office at Salpêtrière, and emptied it on to Bergson's book. He was going to build a structure over *Creative Evolution*. He sat down next to the pile and looked it over. His first thought was whether to consider it as a book beneath blocks, or blocks upon a book. It seemed a rather inconsequential thought but the fact that it had occurred to him gave it some significance. It was an opening thought. He began to pull from the pile and build a wall. To build a wall around a book was to imprison an idea. He felt a tinge of misanthropy and self-doubt. But then encapsulation was not necessarily imprisonment. It might be protection. Circumstances would define it.

As he pondered Sophia's account, he imagined that his structure was the Central Station that she had described. The doorless and windowless walls rose high, and were covered by a flat roof. He built an arch above one face and even had a wooden ball to balance upon it. He surveyed his work. There was pleasure in knowing that it contained a hidden book, a trove of information obscured by appearances.

The Central Station—the place of dreams. He wondered again about what would differentiate the dream world and the waking-state of consciousness in a person who was not technically asleep. If Dr. Roget was wrong in his diagnosis of schizophrenia, which he intuitively suspected, then what was it?

He had never met Sophia before she was admitted, and knew next to nothing about her. What little he had gleaned from her parents suggested a normal upbringing with no particular childhood traumas. They knew very little about her adult life as an artist. She probably kept it from them. She had been involved in Dada from its inception in Switzerland, and in Surrealism in Paris thereafter.

He got up and searched the bookshelf for the Surrealist Manifesto. He knew he had a copy somewhere. He had always been interested in Surrealism. André Breton's statement that poetry was not just writing but a state of being, had made him think that this was an art movement unlike any other. The loss of confidence and respect in the status quo which had allowed such a terrible war, was fertile ground for radical departures.

He found what he had been looking for—a thin and brittle edition of *La Révolution Surréaliste* from 1924. He hadn't looked at it since then.

ENCYCLOPEDIA. Philosophy. Surrealism is based on the belief in the superior reality of certain forms of previously neglected associations, in the omnipotence of dream, in the disinterested play of thought. It tends to ruin once and for all other psychic mechanisms and to substitute itself for them in solving all the principal problems of life.

Lavoisier flipped back and forth between the pages. Breton was certainly loquacious.

Surrealism does not allow those who devote themselves to it to forsake it whenever they like. There is every reason to believe that it acts on the mind very much as drugs do: like drugs it creates a certain state of need and can push man to frightful revolts.

He dropped *La Révolution Surréaliste* on the floor beside the Central Station.

Snippets of conversation returned from the night before. Vivian had been talking about Stone Age tribes whose people did not distinguish reality from dream. Alphonse thought that went hand in hand with intoxicating drugs and animistic beliefs.

A realisation was forming. Not the flash of an epiphany but a steady trickle. Though he disagreed with Roget's diagnosis, he could not completely write it off. He too had considered acute depression and mania, yet his intuition told him that some external factor was involved. His train of thought was interrupted by the doorbell. It was an annoyance as he had not intended to speak to anyone that day.

"My apologies for arriving unannounced, Doctor."

Alphonse stood before him, tall and thin, in the same clean but slightly threadbare suit he had worn the previous night. He had no overcoat. There was an awkwardness between them.

"It's nothing. Come in. And please call me Étienne."

Alphonse had taken him up on his offer sooner than expected. They went into the study. Étienne saw him glance down at the building on the floor.

"That's the Central Station."

"Is Sophia inside?"

"No. Just a book by Henri Bergson. Do you know Sophia?"

"Quite well. That's why I'm here."

Étienne had been grappling with the moral issue of how much, if anything, to divulge about his patient. As Alphonse was a close friend of hers, it didn't seem quite so bad. It still bothered him but he needed help.

He told him how Sophia had been arrested in the Gare du Nord and brought to the hospital by the police. She was being treated by himself and Dr. Roget. He described her account of the journey to the Central Station, and of how she slipped in and out of lucidity.

"I'm coming to the opinion that her psychosis was drug induced. Perhaps a rare reaction. But I don't know what drug, and I can't run tests when I don't know what I'm looking for. Probably too late now anyway. Ibogaine is a possibility. It's readily available."

Alphonse listened intently while his eyes searched the room. He told Étienne that he shared a studio with Sophia.

"She always seemed completely sane, up until about ten

days ago. You know, I think the drug that you are looking for might be found in certain mushrooms."

"What kind of mushrooms?"

"Wild mushrooms. I'm not sure what kind. They grow all over the place. Though I've never heard of them driving anyone mad."

Étienne was scrawling in his notebook.

"Interesting. Tell me, do you consider yourself a Surrealist?"

"No. I don't join movements."

"What about Sophia?"

"Surrealism is at heart a secret society. She's a member, if only a minor one. Her name in the movement is Surrealist in the All-at-Once."

The details emerged of how Sophia might have ingested mushrooms. Étienne wanted to know more about Devereux and his séances.

"They aren't séances. They are performances of ritual magic—not communications with the dead. Communications with the non-existent perhaps."

Étienne jotted it all down. What were rituals if not prescribed forms of speech and action? There was an opinion that all of life was a ritual to some degree—a sliding scale with pure technology on one end, ritual on the other and everything falling somewhere in between.

"What's the point of it all?"

"It's an artistic performance. The audience decides what the point is."

"Have you ever attended one of these performances?"

"No."

Étienne was at his desk. Alphonse sat across from him in the chair usually occupied by his clients. He didn't go for a couch like Freud, he preferred more direct contact. And anyway, he had heard that the only reason Freud had his patients lie on a couch was because he did not want to have to look at them. It could be true, or it could be a joke, or it could be both.

"I'd like to meet this man."

"Well that's unlikely. He has always been reclusive but now he is unreachable."

"I see. Well, I'm trying to help Sophia but I don't know much about her. Could you describe her to me? Just whatever comes to mind."

"I'd say that she is driven, lithe, matter-of-fact, kind, ruthless, unconsciously dishonest, fun. How's that?"

His string of adjectives could well be a description of himself. 'Unconsciously dishonest' jumped out. It presented an interesting paradox. Could you be considered dishonest if you were unaware of your lies? He had trouble reading Alphonse, who appeared to be a tangle of contradictions beneath a calm exterior. Not unlike most people, but in Alphonse's case the contradictions seemed more stark, as angular as his physique. His supreme indifference heightened his charisma. His toleration of others suggested an empathic self-centredness. Depressive but not depressed. A spartan lifestyle accompanied by a sensuous eroticism, or so he had heard. A pathological reserve coupled with free-spiritedness. But how free? Etienne sensed a burden.

"Interesting. A fun game—this stream of consciousness. Not unlike the way surrealists work, don't you think?"

Étienne was suddenly overcome by panic. The telephone was ringing outside in the hallway. He fought off a wave of nausea and felt his chest tighten. He was going to have to do some self-analysis to understand this neurosis. He had been putting it off, which was part of the problem. Despite its obvious uses, the telephone filled him with dread. Its authoritarian intrusion could occur at any time without warning, causing him a high level of stress. He sat frozen in his chair letting it ring incessantly, until it suddenly ceased. The silence was like the aftermath of an accident—stillness rippled by shockwaves.

"Doctor, are you unwell?"

"No, no. I'm perfectly fine thank you. It's just that... I'm not particularly fond of the telephone."

Alphonse gave no response, then abruptly changed the subject.

"I was wondering, do you have any playing cards?"

"I think so."

Étienne fumbled in his desk drawer. It was a relief to be doing something. He found a dog-eared pack.

"Here you are. What game did you have in mind. Or is it a magic trick perhaps?"

"A game of chance. I thought we might compose a few bars of music together."

Alphonse took the cards out of the box as he spoke, and began separating them in suits.

"Filtered chance really, not completely pure. It will generate the notes, but we will use limitations to make them conform to the staff. It's a strange thing—chance. Except when it is used as a verb, it is always referred to as a singular noun. In the plural it has a completely different meaning. Like water in an ocean. Is it one thing or many? I think chance is a number of things, which differ slightly for each person."

He suggested that they compose a melody on the treble clef. They would use the key of C major, for the sake of expediency, to avoid the extra work of sharps and flats. He favoured triple time, on a whim. From the separated suits he took thirteen cards.

"We will use Hearts as notes. The Ace is middle C, and the Eight of Hearts is the C an octave above it. We'll dispense with the rest. Clubs will represent note and rest values. The Ace being the Breve, up to the Five, which is the Semiquaver. Let's make our melody from fourteen notes—the number of letters in *La Gare Centrale*. That would seem fitting."

He spread out the cards on the floor in two distinct piles and shuffled them by rubbing his hand over them vigorously. Étienne got up and came around his desk.

"I see you are not using the royal cards."

"Of course not. This is a republic."

Alphonse pulled a coin from his pocket and held it up between thumb and finger.

"This is our last filter. It will determine whether we write a note or a rest. Heads are notes, tails are rests. Are you ready? You go first."

Étienne flipped the coin in the air, caught it and slapped it down on his wrist. Tails. The first note was silence. He was slightly disappointed. Alphonse was waiting with a pencil and paper.

"Now you have to pick a card from the Clubs pile to determine the value."

Three of Clubs—a quaver rest. Alphonse recorded it on the staff and reshuffled the pile. The game continued.

When they had their fourteen notes, Alphonse looked at the paper, then sang the melody. His voice was surprisingly beautiful and his pitch near perfect.

"My word. You have a lovely voice. I had no idea. And to whom should we credit this masterpiece?"

Alphonse gave a thin-lipped smile.

"I would say it is the melody from 'The Central Station' by Nadja Chance. Tell me Doctor, would it be possible for me to visit Sophia at the hospital?"

"I'm afraid not. She is under guard and the police want to question her. No visitors allowed. The officer in charge believes she is involved in some clandestine anarchist conspiracy. It seems ridiculous to me. Delusional, verging on paranoia. I think that officer could benefit from analysis. Not from me though."

"What's the name of this policeman?"

"Inspector Labeau."

Étienne looked down. On the floor, there was now *La Révolution Surréaliste*, a building containing a book by Henri Bergson and thirteen playing cards.

He was on the right track.

17

Vivian spent the afternoon in her studio with Étienne. It was his second day off work. He stood naked in front of her while she sketched him.

He was not the most remarkable of lovers but there was something different about him. Who else could have come out of the Great War thinking that people were basically good? He had a kindness that was deep and natural.

Alphonse's tolerance for others was founded on the premise of leaving people alone. Étienne's was based on love.

She could not help but compare them. It was something she had a feeling she shouldn't do, but did anyway. In this triangular relationship of theirs, she was the apex. It was because she was more intimately connected to the two of them than they were with each other. That was perhaps why she had wanted them to meet—to make the triangle real, rather than just an imagined shape, privy to her alone. Then of course there was her husband Charles. She supposed the relationship was actually more rhomboidal than triangular. It was a rhombus that just looked like a triangle. That was how Alphonse would have put it.

She uncorked a bottle of wine and poured herself a glass.

"Do you want one?"

"Never before five."

He was governed by his petty principles. She always found it slightly annoying but respected it also, for it was that unassuming self-control which gave him confidence and optimism, so different from her. She agreed with Charles and his friends that the political situation in Europe would fester into another war and she felt a growing sense of hopelessness. It was never far from her thoughts and she often felt tinged with sadness as she looked at the faces of children, or the peaceful and timeless beauty of the sun setting over a field. Most people didn't see it yet, which almost made it worse. She wondered if all her love affairs and her dabbling with art were just retreats into escapism. With his patient curiosity, Étienne encouraged her to get to know herself. It seemed like a rare and valuable gift. She could discuss anything with him without fear of moralizing, or judgement, or even advice. He would listen with a keen expression and never interrupt. "I can't separate joy from grief," she had told him once and he had just looked up from his notebook and smiled.

Despite standing still for so long, Étienne seemed invigorated. It must have been the love they had shared. She wanted to hear him tell her that but she was disappointed.

"Alphonse paid me a surprise visit this morning. He has a beautiful voice."

Vivian felt a stab of jealousy. Alphonse had obviously charmed him, as he did everyone. It was a surprising quality in a person so reserved and private. Alphonse could pass her in the street and act as if they had never met. Maybe the real reason she had introduced him to Étienne, was to let him know that there were other fish in the sea. But by introducing them, she had excluded herself. She rose to put on her clothes.

"Art class is over for the day, Doctor. I have to be somewhere this evening and I need to get ready."

"I imagine that could take some time."

He was obviously trying to make a joke. She found it patronising.

"You wouldn't know. You don't have to play hostess at embassy parties."

Their moods were out of kilter. She had been irritated all day and was not sure why. Étienne seemed flippant with her, which was quite unlike him. It only increased her sense of feeling trapped. It was as if they were in a waiting room together. He was about to set off to Fairyland and she was to board the Titanic. Maybe this relationship had run its course.

"Get dressed. We have to leave."

18

Since returning to the hospital and finding out what had happened behind his back, he had been in a state of silent but alert hostility with Dr. Roget. Étienne feared that his more gentle approach to the subtleties of medicine was no match for Roget's rapaciousness. The veneer of professional respect that had allowed them to ignore their differences, had cracked. Roget portrayed his failure as success. The patient had improved—she was no longer raving. He had made the right decision, and would continue with a course of insulin shock treatment. He had been administering doses to come up to the correct level. Étienne had managed to put a stop to that. A small victory which helped offset his own feelings of ineffectiveness.

Soon after Dr. Roget's ill-fated decision, the police had lost interest in Sophia. The guard had gone from her door and the hospital staff were no longer inconvenienced by Inspector Labeau. He had vanished without another word. Whatever threat they had supposed her to be had been chemically neutralized and their presence was no longer necessary.

Over six weeks, Sophia's condition had improved slightly. She had begun to talk again intermittently and it rekindled his hope. One of her recurrent themes was blindness. He wondered if she was trying to tell him that she had lost her sight, and he tested her eyes. He could find nothing wrong. If she was blind, it was a psychosomatic condition. Perhaps it could be reversed if he was able to help her in other ways.

He was not sure if the responses she gave him were in fact responses, or if they were more a commentary on some tangential reality, only vaguely related to his questions.

She did not improve beyond that, having reached a plateau where she stayed. Étienne had no idea what to do. Whenever he looked at her, he saw the baby at her mother's breast, the curious toddler, the creative young woman. He felt her loneliness. It was a shock to see her this way, as if he had stumbled upon the body of someone he knew. He felt responsible, through his actions and inactions. It left him sad and with a sense of inadequacy. He just did not have the qualities needed to face the savagery of life and persevere. He could never inure himself to suffering.

He tried to hide his lassitude at work. Roget had moved on to new patients without remorse. Sophia's parents decided to remove her from the hospital and place her in a nursing home in Neuilly. One day an ambulance took her away.

The months passed but Étienne still thought about her often. So in early June he decided to visit her. When he arrived at the nursing home he was led out into the garden. He recognized her familiar shape in the wheelchair next to a bench.

Sophia was listening to the ocean and the waves breaking on the rocks below, when she heard a horse approach from behind. The saddle creaked as the rider swung his leg over it. The leather gave off an odour which reminded her of the smell of a book she had once owned, an English book—*The Book of the Dead* by E.A. Wallis Budge. Some books smelled of shit—the old ones with the leather bindings, but not this one. It was musty. She could tell the rider was a man by the weight of his footfall. He came around to face her.

"May I join you?"

She recognized his voice.

"I am blind now, but I remember you. We met once and you gave me some advice."

She was more talkative, which was promising.

"What made you go blind?"

"I saw too much. Too much at once. I thought you were in Paris."

"I was, but I came here to visit you."

"Why would you do that? I am now where you once were, a place you so desperately wanted to leave. You became someone else to do it. And now you're back. Were you captured?"

"That man you met in Paris, who claimed to be me was surely an impostor. You see Madame, the burden of great men is that they loom large in the imaginations of halfwits and metaphysicians, with unforeseen consequences. I have never left this place, as much as I would like to."

He had sat down next to her. She could feel him spread his legs apart.

"I ride out here everyday when I can. I look down for a ship that never comes. When I saw you I was happy, as a new face is a breath of air on this rock. Life here is tedious. I amuse myself by gardening and practical jokes, and small acts of resistance."

Sophia wasn't in the mood for conversation but he did not seem to notice or care. She sensed a petrified forest beneath the churning waves below her.

"My doctor says the air is bad on this island. It has a damaging effect upon the liver. I am curious, Madame—why did you come to such a forsaken place? Were you brought here against your will?"

"There was a chess game. I was dressing up my foot as a handsome soldier. My foot does not belong to me. I don't know whose it is."

"I take it then, that you did not come here of your own volition. Who would? Exile is a poison to the soul. One is left with nothing but memories and even they are curtailed. I shudder to think of what I once was, and what I am now. I used to be the most daring of generals, my life was a romance. Now my only company is a parrot. So you see, Madame, I am glad to discover that you are an exile too."

"I am not an exile. I am a shard of light."

Sophia was not going to get the treatment she needed at this place. But it was beyond his control now. Her parents had said as much by removing her from the hospital. Maybe he had been wrong all along and their lack of confidence was justified. But on the train ride back to Paris, the despondency that had plagued him for the past few months, was pushed aside by his natural curiosity.

She seemed to be exhibiting signs of the Cotard Delusion, that mysterious delirium of negation, where the self was dislocated from the body. It was a fascinating condition with far reaching implications for the concept of selfhood, currently beyond the limits of science. Thinking about it could keep him occupied for years.

By the time he got home, he was in a better mood. He was happy with his career as a doctor. To be able to pursue his interests for the sheer pleasure and excitement of it, and to benefit others in the process, was a high calling. He was lucky.

He never saw Sophia again.

19

October 11th 1942

Ferdinand left the Gestapo headquarters and walked along Avenue Foch towards Rue Pergolèse. Things were going well. This new regime was no less corrupt than previous ones but corruption had never bothered him. It was the natural state of affairs.

The Occupation had been lucrative. Once he had familiarized himself with the new bureaucracy his life was not much different than before. His knowledge of the Parisian underworld made him invaluable to the Germans.

He had just come from a meeting with Standartenführer Knochen. It was partly a commendation for his efficiency, and a briefing in which new responsibilities were laid out. Knochen had invited him up to the third floor, which he might have considered an honour had he been impressed by such things. The meeting had gone well. Still, he was glad to be out on the street again.

Turning left on to Rue Pergolèse, he noticed a familiar face near the intersection with Rue Lalo. It was Devereux talking to someone on the corner. What a stroke of luck.

When he had learned that Devereux had escaped the blaze, he had searched for him relentlessly but the magician had always managed to stay one step ahead. Seeing him again, stirred up some old emotions. He was going to enjoy this. Without hurrying he continued towards him.

As he walked, memories of those pre-war years came back. Alphonse had fled to New York. Sophia had been more fascinating but now she was a vegetable in a mental institution. It was his dislike of artists that had attracted him to them. Their posturing and naive self-importance seemed inconsequential compared to what he did now—mostly finding people for the Germans. There was a cunning satisfaction to hunting down prey. Though his horizon had broadened, he had not been able to forget Devereux. The humiliation he had undergone was still an open wound. Things would never be set right until he had exacted his revenge, and now miraculously, here was his opportunity.

As he got closer to the intersection, he saw that Devereux had noticed him too and broken off the conversation. Then he raised a hand in greeting. It was a mocking gesture. Ferdinand felt his heart beating with angry excitement. He slipped his hand inside his jacket to unholster his gun.

Too late he realised his mistake. The greeting was not for him. It was a signal to two men, who stood up from behind a car. They had been waiting for him. With almost a spasm of embarrassment he knew that he had been beaten at his own game. He saw it all with a sickening clarity. They were just boys. He could see their grim determination and recognized their weapons—a Sten gun and an MP 40. One provided by the British, the other no doubt stolen from a German. His heart was pounding. There was nowhere to run. There was no time left. He didn't want to die.

WITNESSES TO THE ASSASSINATION OF POLICE
INSPECTOR LABEAU MUST COME FORWARD.
ANYONE FOUND TO BE WITHHOLDING
INFORMATION WILL BE SHOT.
BY ORDER OF THE COMMANDANT OF PARIS.

The notice was written in German with a French translation beneath it, and was securely pasted to the wall. Étienne stood back. The message frightened him. As much as he abhorred violence, he wasn't sorry to learn of Labeau's killing but he feared for the innocent people who would suffer for it. His own occasional work for the Resistance, providing clandestine medical aid was always a worry, though he did what he could. It put him at great risk. He didn't know whether it made him safer or not to live so close to the sinister police headquarters, nestled on a residential street.

The last two years had been hard. He had lost his job at Salpêtrière and his private practice had dwindled. Roget had sided with the collaborators and forced him out. These days he spent a lot of time walking. It was better than sitting at home all day. He had just set out to visit the church of Saint-Eustache when he had seen the notice. It would take him just over an hour to get there by foot, and now the peace it would afford him seemed all the more urgent.

He was not religious and had turned away from Catholicism when still a boy, but he had never lost his interest in churches. It was a relief to step into Saint-Eustache. Beautiful old buildings had a permanence that allowed him hope. This horrible war was just an aberration. Life would win out in the end. He could imagine crowds of people thronging the narrow gothic streets outside the church in times gone by.

His echoing footsteps on the stone floor made him conscious of his place in history—one unknown person among many, a feeling of separation and belonging.

He walked down the nave towards the chancel and sat down in one of the pews. He loved the architecture, a mixture of different styles—gothic, classical, and renaissance. Huge columns reached up and fanned out into the vaulted ceiling. He let his head tilt back and gazed upward. The ribbing reminded him of bone. Sitting in this church was like being inside a skull. He used to come here with Vivian before they had drifted apart. He had heard that she was back in England with her husband, leaving just two days before the Germans had arrived. He thought of Sophia in the nursing home at Neuilly and wondered if she was still there. Alphonse had suggested that her madness was a work of art. She had abandoned canvas and paper for the medium of her own mind. She was taking surrealism to its logical conclusion, if that was not an oxymoron. It was an interesting idea, but that is all it was—an idea. It did not account for her suffering and the ruination of her life. It was easy to forget real people when seduced by ideas.

He straightened his head. On the altar in front of him, was the image of the deity. It had fascinated him when he was young and still did. There was so much he had never understood, like the Holy Quintet. Today it sounded to him as if it were a group of five musicians but when he was a child he had accepted it as a truth—an incomprehensible truth. But what was it? The five aspects of God? And what were they? No one really seemed to know, including the priests who acted as if they did. Perhaps God was five musicians. The thought amused him. The image on the altar had a powerful attractive quality. It drew the eye. It had been drawing eyes for millennia. As he looked at it now he searched for its meaning but nothing was readily apparent. Maybe that was the point, the underlying message of religion—a mystery should always remain impenetrable.

Before him was a one-armed, hermaphrodite goblin, seated on a five-legged stool, resting on what appeared to be a bed of fungus.

FIN

Warfilm

A Novella

Scene 1

He was an ordinary German—about thirty-five years old—walking one night on a Berlin street near where he lived, when a car turned the corner and followed alongside him at a crawl. He was alarmed. It was obviously the police and he felt guilty of something.

He was trying to think what he might have done wrong or what he might have been accused of, when the car stopped and two men got out and took him by the arms.

"Franz Leis?"

"Yes."

They pushed him into the back seat. One of them got in beside him and they drove away.

2

The healthier prisoners of the new *Arbeitslager* were kept busy. A ragged group was returning from a work detail and shuffled past an SS guard. He held a mace in his gloved hands.

Among them was a man, a head taller than the rest but just as skeletal. He tried to shrink down into himself as he walked. But even as he stooped, the pink triangle on his striped rags was plain to see.

A cold wind blew through the camp.

3

CONFIDENTIAL

From :- Technical Intelligence Section,
Headquarters Mediterranean Allied Air Forces.
To :- S/Ldr. D. Noyes
Field Intelligence Unit,
c/o 2771 Squadron, R.A.F. Regiment. Date :- 25 March 1945.
Ref :- M.A.A.F./S.

A copy of a letter received from H.Q. (Unit) M.A.A.F.,
re your driving permit, is forwarded for necessary
action please.
G.D.R.P. FENTON Flight Lieutenant, Technical Intelligence
Section, H.Q., M.A.A.F.

COPY

From :- H.Q. Unit M.A.A.F.
To :- C.I.O. H.Q., M.A.A.F., C.M.F. Date :- 23 March 1945.
Ref :- M.A.A.F./CC/2745/1/P.1.
Squadron Leader D. Noyes (83377)

It is understood that the above-named officer drives
American vehicles held on charge by the American M.T.
Pool, and holds a permit to drive issued by the Americans.
It would be appreciated if you could obtain the particulars of the American Officer who issued the permit, and
forward to this office please.

(W.H. WELLER)
for Wing Commander, Commanding.
H.Q., (Unit) M.A.A.F., C.M.F.

4

Noyes liked to let his leg dangle out of his Jeep as he drove. At night he dreamed of corpses in various stages of decomposition. He was very pleased with himself about the Jeep he had managed to wangle from the Americans. It had arrived on Crete by ship two days after him and Purvis, and three days before their kits. News of their arrival had preceded them and a crowd had gathered in the harbour. British officers were not a common sight on the island and were viewed as personal representatives of the King and Mr. Churchill.

Noyes tripped on a coiled rope while disembarking and tumbled into the sea. He had no clothes with him other than what he was wearing, and had to strip naked and be wrapped in a blanket. He found the embarrassment excruciating. It did not take them long to arrange for a billet in a house close to the shore. The owner, Mrs. Zombanakis, an elderly widow, was very happy to see them. She said that British officers were vastly preferable to the Italians and Germans, who until recently she had been forced to suffer. She told them that one German used to shit in his boot every day and make her clean it out. Noyes, who had never even considered shitting in either of his shoes, was at a loss for words.

5

The road up to the villa was steep. Ariadne could feel it in her calves. Her period was late and she wondered if she was pregnant. It was not a good time to have a child. There was not enough food, the Germans had taken it all. Babies were dying. If she was pregnant, she wondered who the father might be, and hoped it wasn't the handsome SS man who shat in his boots.

She was carrying a jar of goat's milk. There were no cows. She hoped it would still be fresh when she reached Lord Strange's house. She worked for him without ever clearly knowing what he paid her for. Was she his personal assistant, or just an errand girl? Perhaps she only had the job because he liked her company. It didn't matter much. The money was good.

When she passed by the cypress trees and crossed the courtyard, he was waiting at the open door.

"Come in, please. I see you've brought milk. How very kind. Thank you."

He was avuncular, slightly heavy in the jowl, with a full head of grey hair. He took the milk from her and motioned her inside.

"Would you like some water? Let's go into the study. It's cooler."

Though it was still only spring, the days had begun to get hot. She took the water and followed him into the study. The shutters were closed and it was pleasantly cool. He sat down at his desk, which had nothing on it but a pipe resting in an ashtray.

"I asked you here because I need a courier."

"Certainly. Where will I be going?"

"Not you, Ariadne. I want you to find me someone suitable."

"What kind of person do you have in mind?"

"Male and German."

"But the Germans have left."

"I'm sure there are still a few about. If anyone can find them, you can."

She was curious to know why he needed a courier. He was as mysterious as his name. She wondered where his loyalties lay. She suspected that he was not completely trustworthy. At least he was not pompous. She could not abide that in a man.

"Might I ask what this courier would be carrying?"

"You might, yes. It's natural enough to be curious. All I can say for now, I'm afraid, is that it's a small object of some sort."

He certainly didn't go in for explanations, but she understood that about him.

"I'll see what I can do."

"I'm sure you will. But please don't take too long about it. Use your charms, Ariadne. Find me a strong, young German and bring him here."

6

The two men who had ushered Franz into the back of their black sedan now ushered him out again. Aside from a few pleasantries, they had not spoken much for the entire journey. They passed through multiple checkpoints where identities were verified and finally entered a complex of low buildings, where they handed him over to men in military uniform who took him inside. He was led down a long corridor with numerous small rooms, in which people were sitting at typewriters and radio sets. His destination was the large conference room at the end. He felt the numbness of a condemned man. In this state of mind, he suddenly found himself in the presence of the Führer. Three other Party notables were also there—Goebbels, Himmler and Bormann, as well as some staff officers. The Leader, who was bent over a map table when he entered, glanced up at him with blue eyes.

"You must be Leis. Good of you to come."

Franz felt some relief. He was off the hook. At least for a few minutes.

"You are probably wondering why you are here."

"I am, Führer."

"We are about to embark on a great venture, Leis."

All eyes in the room were on the Führer. Franz felt honoured that this great man's attention was directed at him alone.

"I am starting production of an epic film."

Things began to make sense. In 1933, while he was working at UFA, Franz was required to fill out and sign a questionnaire. It mostly dealt with racial purity issues and political affiliations. He had been in the clear—one hundred percent German, on both sides of the family with no record of undesirable political association. Everyone who worked in the film industry had to complete this form, which was filed at the Reich Film Chamber.

They would know everything about him and the films he had worked on such as *SA Mann Brand*, *Bleeding Germany*, *The Blue Angel*, and *Hans Westmar*. They would also know about his work with Riefenstahl on *The Triumph of the Will* and on *Olympia*. Franz was proud of his resumé.

"This film will be so sweeping in scope that Hollywood will look like a kindergarten class in comparison. The main problem with their cinema, aside from being run by Jews, is that America is so lacking in culture. They have three or four Negro songs and they keep making films about them. They do it well enough but in the end, so what? German culture is so much richer. If you consider that fact, along with the new film grammar I have invented, where reality and the motion picture are indistinguishable, you can see, Leis, that we will have a masterpiece on our hands. It will be Art that resounds through generations."

There were smiles and nods of agreement all round. Franz could not help being mesmerized by the way he was opening and closing his fist as he spoke.

"Just making this film will be an act of purification for the soul of the Fatherland. But let's get down to business. You have a small part to play in this, Leis. We are aware of your abilities, which is why you were chosen. These are your instructions. You will secure a hearse and a wooden coffin, nothing too elaborate. A prisoner will be delivered to you and you will kill him with a firearm that will be provided. You will put the corpse in the coffin and seal it. You will then drive across the border into France and make your way to Paris as quickly as possible, where you will meet me personally beneath the Arc de Triomphe. You don't have to be concerned about camera position, you will be filmed from every conceivable angle. Just drive. You will be issued an expense account to cover necessary costs. You will submit receipts with written explanations for all disbursements. From now on you will receive further details and instructions from Dr. Goebbels' office. Is that understood?"

"Yes, Führer."

"Good. This is a *Führerbefehl*."

Franz knew that a *Führerbefehl* was not something to take lightly.

"Might I ask one question?"

"I believe you just did."

Franz smiled meekly at the joke.

"Go on then."

"Will we ever see inside the coffin? If we don't, I could load it with sandbags and we wouldn't need a body."

A sudden look of irritation flared up in the Leader's face. His jaw tightened.

"There are greater minds than yours at work here, Leis. Your job is only to obey. Now get out."

A droplet of spittle landed on Franz's cheek.

7

S/Ldr. D. Noyes
M.A.A.F. Field Intelligence Unit
Crete, 31st
March, 1945.

Dear Gilbert,

Your letter of March 25th reached me yesterday. I had no idea they were taking so long to get here. Anyway, thanks very much, particularly for the trouble you and Feldman have taken with the dishing out of Report No. 23. The diagrams for report No. 24 have not yet been completed so hang on for a short while and before long I will send the necessary instructions for dealing with this one.

Referring now to your para. 5 and the letter M.A.A.F./ CC/2745/1/P.1. of March 25th, I'm sorry this matter got overlooked but you know the usual business of being on the job or the road or the typewriter from dawn to dusk. Anyway, the particulars required are as follows:

Motor vehicle operator's permit No.52
Organisation: Technical Intelligence, Hq. M.A.A.F. Adv. Station: APO 650, New York.
Place: APO 650, New York.
Name: Daniel Noyes
Rank: Squadron Leader
Organisation: Hq. M.A.A.F.
Type vehicle: passenger car, cargo trucks, 1/4
Date: February 1st, 1945
Authentication: C.F. Gudrun, Capt.

W/Cdr. Shilltowe mentions that in your letter to him of March 21st you referred to an A.D.I.K. Report No. 231 enclosed. Unfortunately it wasn't. Have you any clue to its whereabouts?

Yet another request. Ask Feldman to look in the file "recognition of German ground radar" and extract all the M.A.P. R.W. photographic reports and photos and send them to me. Any others that come in should be sent immediately. Incidentally, can you find out for me please why and when I was mentioned in dispatches. I am curious and not a little amused. If there is a London Gazette date available, I would very much appreciate the particulars. As for oak leaves, my final request tonight is for you to ring up the camp commandant and ask him if he has any.

Yes, that really is all for now. Kind regards, we expect to see you up here one of these fine days.

Yours, DN

P.S. When the stencilled version of Sigs. Report No. 23 is ready, would you send an additional copy to A.I.2(g) for the attention of F/Lt. Nutting wherever he may be. I would also like an extra copy up here. Nutting, MacBean and Shorter have, of course gone on Weller's party. W/C Proctor spoke in his letter to Shilltowe of his having had them "specially fattened up". And please could you send me some rolls of 35 mm film as my supplies are running low.

8

All the prisoners had numbers tattooed on their arms. The tall man had been assigned 0731602. As a stubborn act of subversion he took ownership of this number by adding its figures and dividing their sum by seven. This gave 2.71428571, which he abbreviated to Two Point Seven. It was a number that reaffirmed his identity by outwitting the authorities at their own game. It was something to be proud of—his own numerical constant.

The guard wore a black leather coat. He gently slapped his gloved palm with the mace as he watched the inmates approach. They unconsciously huddled together. Suddenly he raised the mace and pointed.

"You."

The group stumbled to a halt.

"Yes you. The big fairy. Come here."

Two Point Seven found himself isolated. The group of prisoners moved away without a backward glance. He felt shunned—as if he had never been among them. He towered above the guard, which he knew did not bode well, but what else could he do? He stood in dreadful silence, his body shaking with cold, awaiting the blow.

"We want you for something. Stay right where you are."

The wind howled. There was barking in the distance. Within minutes a vehicle pulled up and Two Point Seven was taken away. It was springtime.

9

A week after his meeting with Adolf Hitler, Franz was summoned to the office of Reichsführer SS Himmler, this time during daylight hours. An orderly served them tea in china cups.
"I would like to congratulate you on being picked for this mission, Leis. It is a very great honour."

Franz carefully placed his cup into the saucer, as if he didn't want to make noise.

"Thank you, Reichsführer."

Himmler turned in his chair and looked out of the window.

"We are having Hitler weather today."

They were indeed. The sky was blue without a single cloud. Warm air and birdsong came through the open window.

"The Führer has this whole film in his mind. It's already a masterpiece."

The Reichsführer took off his glasses and put them on again.

"I'm a busy man, Leis, so I'll be brief. Do you understand what it means to be German?" He paused, but not long enough for an answer, which was a relief for Franz.

"If you wish to know your direction you need to know where you are coming from, don't you agree?"

"Yes, Reichsführer. Absolutely."

"To understand what it is to be German, it is essential to know the true history of our people and not the apologia taught in the Weimar era. Modern science has opened new doors to the future and it has also shed a much brighter light on the past."

Franz shifted his position. He had a deep scepticism for authority but knew better than to express it. Frequent beatings as a schoolboy had taught him that there was no moral superiority to power. He feared it but did not respect it and as a result felt entitled to do whatever he wanted as long as he could get away with it.

"The first people who could truly be described as human were of the Nordic race. They were a strong people, with a naturally sharp intellect. Completely pure and unsullied. Their existence, filtered through time, has reached us today as myth. What you may not realise is that this myth is an echo of reality. Odin and Thor existed. They were the early chieftains of the Germanic people. Forbears to our own Führer, you might say."

"Heil Hitler."

"Yes, yes. Sit down, Leis… . As surprising as it may seem, our ancestors had a much more advanced technology than we do. Thor's hammer was a real weapon. This has been scientifically proven. It is our duty to rediscover their lost knowledge. If we are successful, no one will be able to withstand us and we will claim our rightful due. We can restore balance to the world."

"Very inspiring words, Reichsführer."

"It is to this end that I have established a scientific institute, called the *Ahnenerbe*, right here in Berlin. It brings together many great minds from different fields—geology, history, linguistics, musicology, and so on. My goal for the *Ahnenerbe* is to compile a true history of our origins and study the ancient Nordic technology. You could also add, in a more metaphysical way, that I hope to reveal the soul of the New Germany, which the Führer mentioned last week. We have many expeditions underway all over the globe, and we are busy here analysing and collating the information being sent back. This is where you can be of help, Leis. I know you have your duties and clear directives from the Führer, however you will be travelling through northern France, an area once populated by our race. So I ask you to keep your eyes and ears open for remnants of this ancient people. You might hear a Germanic-sounding folk melody or see a runic-looking inn sign or even architectural remains. Perhaps you might notice some linguistic anomaly. Observations like these, coming from multiple sources, help us here in the Fatherland to construct a bigger, more detailed image of our past. It is crucially important. Can I consider you on board?"

"Most definitely, Reichsführer. I'd be happy to help in any way I can."

"That's good to hear, Leis. I knew I could count on you. You are dismissed. Good luck."

The interview ended with the clinking of china.

10

After Ariadne had left, Lord Strange took the jar of goat's milk and poured it down the drain. He returned to his study and sat down at his desk. He took a key from his waistcoat pocket and unlocked one of the drawers. He fished around with his hand and pulled out a metal container, no larger than a matchbox, which he toyed with between his fingers before setting down. He got up again and went into the kitchen, reaching under the sink for some twine and a scrap of oilcloth. He carefully wrapped the small box with the oilcloth, and tied it securely with the string. Then he locked it back up in the drawer and replaced the key in his pocket. The whole operation took less than ten minutes. He did it in silence, as he was not the kind of person who spoke to himself.

11

Franz was beginning to feel excited about his upcoming trip. He had never left the borders of the Fatherland before. He also anticipated a boost in his career which was bound to come from this opportunity, if he handled it correctly. 1940 was going to be a good year.

He had been busy since getting his orders. He had activated the expense account and rented a garage in which to make his preparations. He had purchased a new Daimler Benz hearse and coffin, along with oil, petrol and extra tyres. He had stocked up on provisions of beer, cigarettes, water and food. All the receipts had been numbered, pasted on blank paper and submitted to the Ministry of Propaganda and Enlightenment with written explanations, as instructed. He had agreed to donate a small percentage of his salary to fund production of a Peoples' Car. He would receive one of his own one day. It was something to look forward to, and he was happy to invest in it. The Ministry had provided him with a Luger and ammunition. Everything was ready. He was scheduled to depart at dawn the following day. All that remained was for him to kill a man. The prisoner was due to be delivered that evening.

He had gone to see his father to say goodbye. His father, Viktor, diligent if slightly bitter, lived above the butcher's shop he owned. There had always been the distance of unshared experience between them. During Franz's adolescence Viktor had been away on the Eastern Front and had been taken prisoner. The Russian Revolution had complicated his release and he had finally returned in 1920, minus three fingers. They managed an unspoken love.

He would have liked to wish his mother farewell too, but she had died eight years before. He remembered her sitting in her chair, knitting woollens for the troops. She would answer him when he spoke but he knew she wasn't listening. He proved it to himself by saying nonsensical things and she never noticed. He also remembered her giving him English lessons. He was a good student, which pleased her no end.

When he left his father's shop that night, he took with him a bucket of blood and offal. The knock on the door came at eight PM. Two SS men delivered the prisoner and left. Now alone with his quarry, Franz stared up at him. He was very tall and thin. The prisoner returned his stare and Franz watched his eyes slide over the Luger on the workbench, to his half-eaten sandwich.

"What's your name?"

"2.71428571 but you can call me Two Point Seven."

"What kind of a name is that?"

"It's a number."

"I've been ordered to kill you."

The prisoner just stared at the wall.

"Are you hungry?"

Franz gave him the rest of the sandwich and he devoured it quickly though not without difficulty. He was missing some teeth.

"I've been instructed to put your body in that coffin over there and drive it to Paris. But I'm going to disobey. I'll fake a shooting for the benefit of anyone listening. You'll have to climb into the coffin. God knows how you're going to fit. They never said you were a giant. I drilled some air holes so you'll be able to breathe. It will be uncomfortable but better than death I think. Tomorrow we'll drive to France and take it from there."

Franz then picked up the Luger and fired a single shot into the wall, then he dipped a cup into the bucket and splattered the wall and floor with its contents. He spent twenty minutes cleaning up the mess he had just made and then he tossed a blanket to Two Point Seven. "Get some sleep. We'll leave at dawn."

12

PERSONAL

Technical Intelligence Section. TECH/INT/VDRPG
Headquarters Mediterranean Air Forces
SQ/Ldr D. Noyes, 6 April 1945.
M.A.A.F. Field Intelligence Unit.

Dear Daniel,

Many thanks for your letter of 31 March. Note time lag now that we are so separated. All your various instructions are being carried out. We are making good the omission of sending report A.D.I.K. No. 231 by enclosing it now. Please return it when you can. We also enclose our file copies of MAPRW photographic reports and photos as you do not seem to have had these although Corporal Feldman assures me that we have forwarded all these to you as they have come in. I sent today 8 X 35 m/m film up to Shilltowe, all that are available at the moment, he will no doubt accommodate you. I sent them all to him before receiving your letter and also assuming that you would all be in touch with one another.

I have not congratulated you officially on your 'mention'. Many congratulations, old man, it is one which is thoroughly deserved, more power to your elbow. I have enquired as to the supply position of oak leaves for you and found that none are available at present. They are on demand however and as soon as they turn up I will send you a bunch!

Caserta is I must admit a great improvement on Cairo but some transport would be a great help. At the moment if you need a car, they ask you your rank and name and are somewhat condescending if you are amongst the lower form of animal life as myself. I have had occasion to go into Naples twice very recently in connection with despatch of equipment to A.M. and other duties, and on each occasion had to waste over two hours going to places with other officers. Off the record too, transport would occasionally break the present monotony of spending each evening in the mess (I have some introductions, very nice, which are just out of range of my feet, a great pity). I still retain my M.E. W.A.A.F prejudice, I'm afraid.

Twenty other bodies of a pioneering nature and myself last Sunday heavily thrust ourselves with much b....y (pardon) sweat and labour up the side of Vesuvius for 2000 feet, to the lip of the crater where we enjoyed the scent of sulphur, and the moisture of mist. There was very little separating me from my final destination on departure from this world. The ground was hot and sulphurous, in fact one type managed to burn his ankle through putting his foot too far in. The descent was mostly sudden, composed largely of what I believe is technically called 'screeing' which to the laity is just missing sliding down on what is more properly used for sitting. It took one and 3/4 hours up and 3/4 of an hour down. After our great adventure we partook of plenty much vino, steak, eggs and chips. A good time was had by all. A number of fellows said afterwards that at half way if the blokes in front and behind had not been moving forward they would have turned back. It was certainly more strenuous than I had anticipated. Still there were no ill effects, in fact I felt remarkably fit the next day, it must have been the vino.

Don't worry about giving me things to do, I am only too pleased to help in any reasonable way possible. I certainly however have been somewhat hectic lately, what with W/Cdr Colrick's work which has taken up quite an amount of time, my visit to Sicily, a request from M.E. which Cedric should have attended to before he left. Cedric is away with Hazell and already apparently much improved in health although he was somewhat ropey when he arrived, his leg still being a bit painful.

He seems to be determined-if he can get out of it-not to return to Cairo and in fact has said all his goodbyes and cleared things up there mostly. This is a matter I wish to discuss with Shilly when I come up. I have also got and propose to bring with me for safety's sake when I come up and see you soon, a watch for you and one for Hugh.

They are in process of making an open-air cocktail bar between 1 & 2 messes, a bulldozer has already flattened the ground, though progress is slow, a small stone dance floor is to be included.

Yours sincerely,
Gilbert.

Please excuse this badly phrased screed but am in haste for mail.

13

Ariadne lived near the harbour, not far from Mrs Zombanakis' house. She had no family. As a baby she had been left to die at the side of a road in Asia Minor when the Greeks fled from Turkey. She was discovered by a peasant woman who lifted her up and held her close. She had lost her own child and recognized that this baby was a gift from God in recompense for what he had taken from her. She raised Ariadne as her own but died suddenly when she was still young. Ariadne was thus twice orphaned. She had made her own way and grown up with the conviction that she had only herself to rely on. She had never married. Though gregarious enough, she had always felt alone. She did not like to be dependent or indebted. It was no great moral obstacle for her to start sleeping with the Italian and German occupiers. She needed to survive and used what was available to her. It was not about pleasure, though it was not always unpleasant. Now that they had gone, she had to be more careful than ever. The partisans in the mountains were rounding up collaborators. This was why she valued her job with Lord Strange so highly. He would protect her and he never required sexual favours.

How was she going to find this German man he wanted? She started by trawling the bars on the waterfront but that led nowhere. There were just no Germans left in the area, they had all retreated to the north of the island. Getting up there would be dangerous. If she had to do it, she would contact an English Major she knew, who spread propaganda, ran spies and retrieved deserters from across the lines. It was not an appealing prospect. She would prefer to stay in the liberated zone. She had heard of the two British officers, newly arrived and staying with that hag Zombanakis. They were not German but her intuition told her that they might be as good a place to start as any, and they might present some new opportunities.

14

Squadron Leader Daniel Noyes and Flight Lieutenant Edward Purvis were both intelligence officers of the RAF. Both were members of the Field Intelligence unit, a part of the Mediterranean Allied Air Forces. Noyes worked in the Technical Intelligence Section, which was staffed by British and American specialist officers, and was responsible for the examination and disposal of captured enemy equipment such as aircraft, signals equipment, bombs and enemy ammunition. Purvis worked in C.S.D.I.C.—Combined Services Detailed Interrogation Centre, the section that was responsible for the interrogation of enemy prisoners of war and appreciation of all enemy documents and prisoners of war's personal effects. It was also responsible for the interrogation of individuals who volunteered information.

There was a third sub-section, the H.Q. Unit, which took care of the briefing of the Intelligence Sections, the dissemination of all reports and the disposal of all captured documents and other material. It would also arrange for the interrogation by C.S.D.I.C. officers of civilians believed to have information of value. Interrogation officers carried a special C.S.D.I.C. pass and interrogation or any other form of contact with prisoners by unauthorised persons, regardless of rank, was strictly prohibited.

Since the Italians had evacuated and the Germans had withdrawn, they had been sent to Crete to examine what had been left behind. They had known each other for some time and had worked together in North Africa so their relationship was quite informal, though Noyes was superior in rank. It was Purvis who Noyes had railed at, when he kept falling asleep at the wheel of the lorry they had filled with nurses when they made their escape from Cairo.

They would usually accompany one another on the examination of sites when a report came in, and though technically forbidden, Noyes would sometimes sit in on interrogations. He had an adequate knowledge of German. On one occasion in North Africa, Purvis was suffering from malaria and Noyes drove out into the desert alone. His target was a downed JU88, reported to be about seventy miles distant. He had been given the correct pinpoint for once and he did not have much trouble finding the aircraft. It lay on its belly in the wasteland. The blades of one propeller on the port wing were bent at right angles where it had impacted the ground. Noyes gathered his tools and climbed in through a gaping hole in the fuselage. The stench of putrefaction was overpowering. He crawled through the wreckage and dead crewmen to the cockpit. There had been a fire. The pilot was still strapped into his seat but no longer had a face. The rest of his head was intact, held together by the leather flying helmet, miraculously unburned. Noyes had to sit in his lap in order to reach the control panels. He began to disassemble the instruments, taking meticulous notes in the book he carried for that purpose. He would usually have taken numerous photographs as well, but his camera had been stolen in Italy and a replacement from England had not reached him yet.

While he carried out his work he scanned the sky and listened for aircraft. There was no cover in the desert. He worked as quickly as he could under difficult conditions but it still took too long. The loneliness was intense. His mind kept wandering. He remembered the time he was called up and had appeared at the recruiting office. There was golf paraphernalia everywhere. Though he personally hated the game, he knew a lot about it as his father had forced him to caddy on weekends. After several well placed observations about golf, Noyes left the room an officer in the RAF.

When he felt he could learn no more, he packed up and made his way back down the fuselage. As he climbed out through the hole, he saw to his dismay that he had been surrounded by a large group of Bedouins. He knew they were not overly fond of the British and that his sidearm would be useless against such numbers, except to put a bullet in his own head. One of them stepped forward and greeted him. He replied in the correct fashion. He had learned some Arabic. The others looked on. The man invited him to share food. He understood that if he refused this hospitality he would likely be left dead with his penis sewn into his mouth, so he accepted graciously. He went with them to their camp. It always amazed him how they were able to blend in and out of the desert. Some time later, after managing to swallow goat testicles without retching, he returned the hospitality with a gift of tea. The Bedouins were envious of the British tea ration and he always saved the leaves when he made a brew, drying them on the bonnet of his Jeep and storing them in a small bag. They were satisfied with the gift and he was free to go.

He climbed back into the Jeep and took off at a brisk pace. He was later than he wanted to be. The desert was silent. Occasionally he heard eerie and inexplicable sounds. The sky was malevolent. The monotony was sickening. There were no landmarks he could recognise. He had nothing to rely on but his compass, his map and his resolve. He hated this place.

He suddenly came across a group of shirtless men playing cricket. He slowed to a stop and saw they were Australians. He was happy to see them. A freckled lieutenant reached out a hand.

"Set your tent up here with us, mate. We've got tucker and plenty of beer."

Noyes explained with some awkwardness that on principle he always set his tent at a distance from other encampments.

"Suit yourself. But come and eat with us."

So he drove a short distance and erected his tent. He unfolded the small camp bed and threw a blanket on it, as nights were cold, then he returned on foot to join the Australians. They were finishing up their game when he arrived. They sat around, sharing their rations and exchanged news of the war. They swapped stories and jokes and, as promised, drank copious amounts of beer.

Much later he staggered back in the dark and threw himself on his bed. He awoke with a jolt, in the early morning, to the howling of Stuka dive bombers. He crawled under the bed and put his hands over his ears. He shut his eyes tightly. There was a metallic taste in his mouth, like copper. He always had that taste when he was afraid.

The attack was over within minutes. He got up and left the tent to survey the damage. The Australians were gone. All that remained were body parts. Blood soaked into the ground. Everything was quiet. Not one person was alive but him. He wept.

15

They left at dawn as planned. Franz drove his brand-new hearse through the morning streets without hindrance. Two Point Seven was squashed in the box. They reached the border in good time but once across it the situation deteriorated. The roads became clogged with traffic. Military vehicles, civilian cars, ambulances, wagons and carts were jammed together, interspersed with horses and pedestrians, all weighed down with bundles, large and small. Everyone was intent on getting somewhere but no one could be certain where that was. They were all in such a hurry. Franz was in a hurry too. He was concerned that he would be late for his rendezvous with the Führer but when he thought about it, no one had given him a specific time. It was unusual that such an important detail had been overlooked.

Every once in a while, a Luftwaffe fighter would fly in low and strafe the crowd. It was all part of the production, Franz thought. They must be getting aerial shots. This new mixture of war and entertainment was a disturbing concept.

By now the road had become completely blocked and nothing was moving except people on foot. He decided to get out of the vehicle and see what was going on. He knew it was futile but he would stretch his legs and ease his frustration. He left Two Point Seven in the back. It was unkind but necessary. He squeezed his way between the cars and then he heard the sound of engines in the sky. He looked up. More raiders were coming in. This time they were dropping bombs. He could see them exploding further down the road. Then he felt grit on his face and was caught in a violent wind. He could not breathe, he was gasping but there was no air. He was pulled from his feet and hurled. He came down moments later with his head on the running board of a horseless cart. Franz opened his eyes. It seemed as if the bombers were settling into the trees like crows. Then he realised he was watching them through the branches as they receded. He got up. His body still worked. He dusted himself off and felt the back of his head. No blood, just a bump. It was miraculous. He looked around for the hearse with a growing sense of panic. It could not be far off but he felt disorientated. He sat back down, then stood up and tried again. There it was, with the long black rear end. He made his way towards it, stopping to suddenly vomit in the ditch. Afterwards, he felt more himself and was better able to take in his surroundings. The carnage was horrible to look at and he kept his gaze averted as much as he could. It was unbelievable that this level of pain and destruction had become acceptable in film production. It never used to be that way. Quite near the car he noticed a small side road, flanked with hedgerows. He would take that. He did not care where it led.

Franz climbed in and started the engine. Everything was functioning normally. He reached back and tapped on the coffin.

"Are you all right?"

He heard some muffled expletives and was satisfied, so he inched the hearse forwards and then drove with two wheels in the ditch, hoping that the tyres and exhaust pipe would survive. When he reached the road he had seen, he turned abruptly and began to feel some relief. The congestion grew lighter, until eventually there was none at all. His map lay open on the passenger seat but he paid it no more attention. Where was he going? Where was it? The harder he tried to remember, the more impossible it became. He should just keep driving and stop thinking about it. But where was it? Paris, that's it. Paris. Thank God. But where was Paris? It did not matter. At least he knew where he was meant to be going. When he was completely clear of the mess behind him, he would find his way there on back roads and lanes.

The sun was getting brighter and the landscape was changing. It was growing more flat and arid. He decided to take a short break and parked at the side of the road. He let Two Point Seven out of the box, stretching and groaning. Franz laid out a napkin on the ground and they picnicked in the dust on bread and cheese with two bottles of beer.

"Tell me, why were you sent to a concentration camp?"

"I painted a picture."

"Is painting a crime?"

"I painted a face with an arsehole for a mouth and a cunt on its neck. I also happen to be a Jewish homosexual and a communist. My forebears were probably gypsies and I enjoy speaking Esperanto. I'm an intellectual too. It's a clear-cut case. But tell me, have you ever been to France before?"

"No. This is my first time."

"So you obviously wouldn't know then."

"Wouldn't know what?"

"That this isn't France."

16

"Good morning, Herr Doktor."

He strolled smartly through the secretary pool, as was his custom when arriving for work, with only a slight limp. He greeted the girls as he passed. He knew what women wanted. They adored him with good reason. He was a dangerously fascinating man, and generous with his attention. An irresistible combination. He paused at the last girl in line.

"Your correspondence and schedule for the day, Herr Doktor."

As he took the papers, he let his hand rest on her shoulder.

"Thank you, Ulrike."

He lifted his hand abruptly and went into his office, closing the door with a snap. His office was tastefully decorated. It was large and comfortable, full of light. On the back of the door was a full-length mirror. He studied himself for a few minutes and was pleased with what he saw—he was crisp and handsome in his uniform, exuding confidence and power, just forty-three years old and head of The Ministry of Propaganda and Enlightenment. He had the most advanced communication technologies in the world at his fingertips. One could barely notice the crippled foot any more. In his youth it had been a source of shame but now he saw it as a blessing. It had kept him apart from a normal life with other children and had led him instead to books and knowledge. It had allowed his genius to flower and had raised him from peasant to Reichminister.

He cut his musings short as it was time to begin the day's work. He glanced at the schedule—an 11:00 AM meeting with Speer, the Führer's new pet. He distrusted Speer. The man was an opportunist, not a true National Socialist, though he was not without talent. His use of lighting at Nuremberg transcended the purely material forms of architecture. He wished he had thought of that himself.

Next, a talk at the ship workers' guild—run of the mill. He turned to his correspondence. There was a letter from his sister Maria. He put it aside, he would read it when he got home. And what was this? A message from Himmler. How he despised that man. So small-minded with his banal mysticism. The note was brief: 'Any news of Leis?'

There had been no news. Leis seemed to have disappeared. He had never reached Paris. The Führer had been justifiably apoplectic. But then again, plans had not quite gone as imagined.

As head of this ministry, it was his responsibility to oversee the Führer's film, including the editing, which was what he enjoyed most. The idea had come to him to release individual scenes as newsreels. The film in its entirety would be assembled later as more footage came in. In the meantime he had a stunning source of ready-made propaganda available to him.

The Doctor put down his papers and went over to the phonograph he kept in his office and chose a jazz record from among his collection. It was forbidden music of course, but then he was the one who had forbidden it. He found it relaxing and it helped him to clear his mind. He loved music, as did the Führer. They were two sides of the same coin. The Führer was the Nationalist and he the Socialist. Together they had forged the Third Reich from nothing.

17

Franz wiped the knife and folded the napkin because he liked to keep things neat. He walked down the road to urinate. When he returned, buttoning his fly, he called out to Two Point Seven to get in the box. There was no answer. He opened the back and looked into the coffin. It was empty. He scanned the horizon. Everything was flat. There was not a bush or tree to hide behind, not a hollow or a hill. He called out again. Silence. He was alone.

He sat in the driver's seat for a while and wondered what to do. He no longer felt so sure of himself. Then he started the car and drove off. He kept driving for several hours and the landscape never changed. He seemed to be going nowhere but eventually the road widened and he entered a small town. There was a colonnaded building to his right that looked like a shady respite from the stark sunlight. In the middle of the road was a large statue of a reclining nude, bigger than his vehicle. He parked and got out to look around. He walked up and down the road. Beyond this hamlet was an expanse of empty desert in both directions. Something was not right. There were no people. Could it be a film set?

He walked around the statue. It was strangely beautiful and white. He went back to the car and took his Luger from the glove compartment and hid it in his waistband. He also took the gold sovereigns which the Ministry of Propaganda and Enlightenment had provided him and wandered over to the building. The covered terrace under the arches looked like a restaurant or café, as it had chairs and tables. A man sat at one of them with his back to Franz. After his experience with the crowds earlier in the day, he had forgotten what a relief it was to see another human. It came as a shock to him, as he mounted the steps, to see that the man was Two Point Seven, drinking coffee from a small cup.

"What are you doing here?"

"Questions, questions... Answers are inextricably linked to questions—joined at the hip—so try answering before you ask. I wonder if you're familiar with the paintings of De Chirico in his metaphysical period."

He put his cup down, brushed past Franz on the steps and loped off into the desert with his lanky stride. Franz watched him get smaller and smaller until he disappeared.

"Come in. Please sit."

He turned. There was an old Chinese man in the doorway with an apron around his waist.

"You would like food and drink? Sit down."

"I would. Thank you."

Franz slumped into a chair. He had not realised how tired he was. The old man went inside. He reappeared carrying a tray, from which he pulled a glass and a cold bottle of water. The condensation slid down its neck and left a faint ring on the table. He produced a basket of bread and a bowl of yogurt. Lastly he set down a half carafe of wine. Then he went back inside.

Franz was no longer in a hurry. He sat and enjoyed his food. It was good. He wished he had someone to talk to or at least a newspaper to read, anything that would connect him to the world. He stared into the empty square. The Chinese man came back with a black woman. They seemed to be married. She looked him over, appraising him unselfconsciously.

"If you are interested in staying the night, we have rooms. Clean and well priced. Come in when you've finished."

It was appealing, especially as he had no idea where he was. He had driven enough for one day. He needed to stay in one place for a while. He didn't know much about De Chirico, and who was Two Point Seven anyway? What did he mean by likening questions to answers?

18

He was trying to think of the quotation that ended "… let the copulation begin." He racked his brain but could not place it. Purvis was out looking for night life. He needed something to break the monotony of his days. This Cretan venture was a non-starter. They had searched the entire liberated zone but the Teutons had been too efficient in their demolition. Thieves and the elements had done for the rest.

He was quite enjoying the war. He'd had some narrow scrapes but managed to pull through unscathed. He liked being out of England, and for a packet or two of cigarettes he could have as much sex as he wanted. Of all the starving people he had encountered, most would choose cigarettes over food. His work as an interrogator was certainly more interesting than his career as a schoolmaster. He had been taken on as a German teacher in the same institution he had attended as a boy, and when the war broke out his knowledge of the language had led him straight to C.S.D.I.C.

Purvis was happy with himself. He did a good job and his conscience was clean. He liked to hit his target. He should have been a fighter pilot. They had all the luck with the girls. That was fair enough he supposed, seeing as how their lives were so tenuous. Here he was—from public school to the island of Crete, in the company of Noyes. Life was an odd thing. So was Noyes. He had known him for some time without ever really understanding him.

He remembered the time in North Africa when he had malaria and Noyes had vanished into the desert for ten days. He had been reported missing in action and given up for dead when he showed up in his Jeep at HQ, demeanour unruffled, though something in him had changed. He would not say what it was. He never discussed his feelings. Then there was the German pilot officer's uniform that he brought back with him. He had quickly squirrelled it away and no one ever saw it again.

As he walked he kept his eyes open for a suitable establishment. There wasn't much to choose from but then he saw something that might fit the bill. It was an ouzo bar, a big open room full of tables at which men were playing backgammon. Strangely enough there were one or two women in there, and that was good enough for him. The customers turned and stared as he entered but forgot about him when he sat down. A waiter arrived and he ordered an ouzo. It came with a saucer of sunflower seeds. He emptied the glass. It tasted like horse piss. He had two more in quick succession.

Ariadne sat watching from a table in the corner. She observed the sandy-haired man cracking seeds between his teeth and knocking back ouzos. He must be one of the newly arrived British officers. She wondered where the other one was. She enjoyed making a rapid analysis of the people she came across. It was an entertaining game and sometimes proved quite useful. This man was handsome, reasonably intelligent looking. He was probably generous but competitive, not too complicated and a womaniser. He would be over soon. Five minutes later he was.

"Mind if I join you? Hate to drink alone, you know." Without waiting for a reply, he pulled out a chair for himself.

"Flight Lieutenant Edward Purvis RAF, at your service. What's your poison?" She ordered a raki.

"Where's your boyfriend?"

"Excuse me?" He was confused for a moment. Then he grinned at her.

"He's otherwise engaged."

Purvis was not averse to using attractive women in his line of work. He had a reputation as an accomplished procurer, of which he was secretly proud. They had cracked a few prisoners that way.

"And what may I call you?"

"Dimitra."

"Cigarette?"

He extended an open packet and lit one for her when she accepted. She sipped her raki and waited.

"Would you like to go dancing, Dimitra? It's rather dull here. Do you know anywhere better?"

She did.

19

Strange stood naked in his dressing room. He practiced an economy of movement and remained quite still. Strange was not his birth name. He was originally Frank Walsingham. Before he left England he had legally changed it by deed poll to Lord Strange—Lord being his first name, with no middle initial. Over time he had systematically erased any history of himself. He had a prodigious intellect and an imagination to match. He used both of these attributes to examine the lives of the people around him. It was a lifelong project, something always enlarged upon that could never be finished, an experiment with infinity. He was building a maze. It was not the type of structure that occupied the physical world. It existed solely in his mind and was constructed from the life-trajectories of others. He visualized it as a diagram of dissecting lines that reached into eternity. He was able to see it clearly and add to it as his fancy commanded. He plotted every move. Sometimes in order to please his aesthetic sensibilities, as if to make a passage turn in a certain direction, he needed to influence events in the outside world. He had a keen sense for weaknesses in people and how to exploit them, and for that purpose he had created a wide network of social connections. He was obsessed with this work. It was a kind of food for him, a source of life. In that parallel existence, regarded by the majority as reality, he ate sparingly. He was a mystery to everyone.

His thoughts were interrupted by a violent rapping on the door. The knocking continued as he dressed, without hurry, and only ended as he opened the door, leaving a fist in mid-air. Outside stood a powerful, wiry man who looked annoyed, as if the act of the door being opened had robbed him of something.

He was dressed in traditional Cretan male attire: knee-high boots, breeches, black waistcoat over a loose shirt with a fringed black kerchief drawn tightly round his skull. He was adorned with weapons.

"Alexis, what a pleasant surprise. We have not met in a long time. What brings you here?"

"I've come for the girl."

Strange was condescending and made him feel like a servant. It was this kind of relationship between peasant and aristocrat that he wished to destroy. He did not understand Strange at all. He knew nothing about him. No one did. All that was available was speculation—he was a British aristocrat who dallied in archaeology, one of those entitled people who believed they had the right to extract the riches from the soil of a foreign country and keep the proceeds. Alexis looked at him with loathing. This man was an imperialist anachronism. His day would soon be done. However his day was not quite done yet as he obviously had ties to the British government, which Alexis still needed. How else could he have provided arms and other assistance in certain matters?.

"What girl are you referring to?"

"The one who works for you. Ariadne."

Alexis was a hard man, made harder by the war. He had seen his village razed and his father executed along with his two brothers. His aims were simple—to kill Germans and to fight to establish a communist state. He had educated himself by reading all the communist literature he could come across. Strange had helped there too.

There was another side to Alexis that made him uncomfortable. He had become a faith-healer. It was not from personal choice. The village from which he and his ancestors had come was a poor place. The villagers had always struggled for survival and doctors were beyond their means. They had always turned to his family for their medical needs. A tradition rooted deep in time had made them healers. It was a gift that had been mysteriously passed down the male line to the present. Now it fell to him, as his father and brothers were dead. His mother had told him that he must step up.

"I am not a healer. I don't know anything about it. I don't even believe in that kind of thing. I am a fighter and revolutionary. I'm an atheist."

"Your opinion is unimportant. You must help your village. The people believe in you. If you don't do that, then who are you?"

So he became the healer for his people without a village. His cures grew ever more effective, even better than his father's, and as this happened he found himself beginning to question his other identity. It was disturbing.

"Why do you want her?"

"She has committed the crime of consorting with the enemy. She must answer to a People's Court."

"You and your cronies, I assume. Well I'm afraid you can't have her."

"We'll see about that."

"We will indeed. Good day."

The door was firmly shut.

20

Dusk was falling. Franz decided to take the woman up on her offer and rent a room. He needed to sleep. The inside of the building was a large open space with a gallery running around it. He could see arched doorways above. There was a kitchen spanning the length of one wall. There he found her preparing food. He gave her one of his sovereigns and she said he could stay for a month. She did not offer change. The old man appeared and led him up the stairs to his room. It was clean and simple. The walls were white with no other decoration. It contained a bed, a chair, a wash basin and a jug of water. There was a large window. He liked it. The Chinese man indicated that the facilities were down the hall.

When he was alone, Franz opened the window and looked out. It was dark but he could see that the ground level was higher this side of the building than at the front. He went out again to retrieve a few items from his vehicle, but when he crossed the square to where he had parked, he discovered that the hearse was gone. He looked up and down the single street and saw nothing. It must have been stolen. Had he not been so tired, he might have been more upset. Instead he just turned and walked back. He went up to his room and slept deeply.

In the morning he looked out of the window again. The ground level this side was definitely higher, which meant the building was set on a hill. That was odd because he had not noticed any hills when he'd arrived. The land had seemed completely flat. He made out a track, winding its way up the slope opposite his window. He continued to puzzle over this mysterious topography while he breakfasted on the terrace—black coffee and bread. Afterwards he went out to look for the car again. It was still missing, so he decided to go and look at the track. But it proved impossible to get there. When he walked to the corner of the building he was suddenly filled with dread and could not bring himself to go further. It was the kind of fear he might feel if he stood on the edge of a precipice. He made several attempts, walking away and then returning. The dread would diminish and then increase. It was the same every time.

He gave up and climbed the big staircase. There had to be an explanation. He sat upon the bed and ran his fingers through his hair. The problem must lie with him. He had never been particularly introspective or anxious but now he seemed to be suffering from agoraphobia. He might be more damaged than he'd thought. In every other respect he felt perfectly well. At least he was not frightened of the window. He would go out that way.

The ground below was not far.

21

Ariadne needed a plan of action but couldn't come up with any good ideas, so she took a walk along the waterfront. She liked the boats gently rocking at their moorings. The water close to shore was dirty with oil, further out it was a pure azure blue. Her feet occasionally disturbed a lizard sunning itself on the crumbling cement. There was a man sitting on the dock ahead of her, his feet hanging over the edge, gazing out to sea. He looked preoccupied and forlorn.

She had enjoyed herself dancing with the British officer Purvis. He was good company. She had managed to resist his advances without offending him and he had intimated, upon parting, that he might be able to give her a job.

By now she had reached the man on the dock. He wasn't a local.

"Are you lost?"

He looked up at her. He obviously could not understand Greek. On impulse she tried again in German.

"Are you lost?"

"You could say that."

"Where are you trying to go?"

"That's part of the problem. I'm not sure. I was trying to go to Paris."

Ariadne couldn't believe her luck.

"Would you like to join me for a coffee, if we can find any? You can tell me your story. Do you speak any other language?"

"I speak English."

"Good. That would probably be better than German right now..."

Franz heaved himself up and they walked off side by side.

22

The Junior School
Brighton College
Sussex

25th March, 1945

My dear Purvis,

Thank you so much for your recent letter—all the more because it tells me that you are still going strong. We still peg away at Brighton though you would find the place somewhat different from the old days. We have been through quite a sticky time and frequently wondered if we were wise to stay put in what was generally assumed to be a danger spot. However the place was never actually hit though on occasion the Hun dropped his load unpleasantly near. At the beginning of the war I was switched over to take charge of what was left of the old B.C. Prep school – actually the numbers were seven boarders and 30 Day Boys all housed in the old Bristol House. In spite of the war atmosphere I managed to increase the numbers steadily and now we have 40 Boarders & 55 Day boys—a close fit!! It is hard work & frequently irritating but I like it, especially as it is an independent command and I am my own master within reasonable limits. My sister keeps house and Miss Fenwick is still with us. Charles Allen still functions but he is within a few months of the statutory retiring age (60) though it is likely that he will see the war through. He leads a worried existence as his third son is a flight engineer in the Pathfinders and the eldest an instructor in the R.A.F. The second son, John, was killed in a bomber some time ago and his death upset C.R.A. considerably.

Hughes, tho' now 62, still teaches but will be glad to give it up when the war ends. We are very lucky in Mr. Heath's successor—A.C. Stuart Clark who is a very live wire indeed and has the needful energy at 38 to put his ideas into force. Owing to the war we have had very little music though last term we had quite a good orchestral concert and another is scheduled for next term. As an Xmas celebration "The Fourth Wall" was very well done and at a very well attended Carol Service there was a collection for the prisoners of war for whom we collected £150. In common with a great many other people, we are hoping that 1945 will see the end of war. It is the school's centenary at which we hope to see as many old boys as possible. You probably have read the Centenary Endowment Appeal with which we hope—rather ambitiously, perhaps—to raise £50,000 for scholarships etc.

It will make all the difference to the prospects of the school if everyone will help according to their means. I hear frequently from various old boys though it is difficult to remember which of them were contemporaries of yours. If you get some home leave, I hope you will find the time to pay us a visit. Till then, Best of luck.

Yours ever
J.L.B. Nokes

23

Ariadne and Franz never found a place that could serve them coffee, so they kept walking and ended up sitting in the dust by some ruins. Franz noticed a name carved in one of the stones. It was beautifully executed and seemed like a lot of work for a mere doodling in rock. It must have taken a long time. Perhaps there was more time available in the past.

– BYRON –

He wondered if it had been carved by the poet himself. The one whose name he recognised but otherwise knew so little about. She said it was.

He told her how he had driven into France with a friend, but not why, and how they had become mired in traffic. How he had turned off the road to find that the crowds had dispersed and the land had become desert. He described how his friend had vanished and how he had arrived in a strange town. He went on to describe the hotel and the theft of his car.

"What do you think?"

Ariadne had no idea what to make of it but she was intrigued. He seemed so earnest that she wanted to believe him, though his story made no sense. She had certainly never heard of the town or hotel he mentioned. She was very familiar with the area. If they existed, she would know about them. She was left in that liminal space between belief and disbelief.

"You should come back with me and I'll show you. They have real coffee."

The decision was easy. He might be just the man Strange was looking for, whether his hotel existed or not. It was funny how things could fall into place so unexpectedly. Aside from that, she found him interesting and wanted to know more. She would soon have proof of whether he was telling the truth or if he was mad, though he seemed quite sane. Something must have happened to him. How could he not know where he was?

He led the way, back to the dock and out of the town, up the hill and on to a track she didn't know about. The air smelled better, imbued with pine and wild herbs. Eventually they arrived outside the window. He gave her a leg up and then pulled himself in behind her. Once inside, he went down the hallway to wash, preferring a tap to the pitcher in his room. He returned to find Ariadne stretched naked across the bed. Her nakedness surprised him, and it made him feel uneasy. He was not used to women who expressed their desires so freely.

As he tore off his clothes, he saw the slight and perfect prominence of her hip bones. She said nothing but lay there with her head back.

Afterwards, she drew on an English cigarette and exhaled. He watched the smoke drift off. Sex brought him peace that he had not felt since the Gestapo plucked him from the street. He brushed some ash away from her shoulder where she had let it fall. He had no idea what she was thinking and she made no effort to enlighten him.

They dressed and went downstairs. They passed by the kitchen where the day's food was laid out in chafing dishes and continued to the terrace, where they sat themselves at a table. The old man approached.

"Can we have some food please?"

Franz had quickly learned that there was no menu in this restaurant. You did not order. You ate what was presented to you. If you liked, you could inspect the food in the kitchen beforehand but beyond that there was no choice. They were given three bowls: white beans, roasted potatoes and vegetable stew. The old man glanced at Ariadne and then at Franz as he served them.

"She your wife?"

"No. We're friends."

"You son of a gun." He cackled.

There were neither plates nor utensils. They ate with their hands, using pieces of bread to scoop food from the bowls. Ariadne licked her fingers.

"This food is wonderful. I haven't tasted anything like it in years. How can it be possible? The war has caused such scarcity."

"There is no war here."

Franz poured them some wine. This place was so calm and silent. It was odd. She wondered why she didn't know about it.

"I work for an English archaeologist. You should come with me and meet him sometime. I'm sure you'd like him. He might even give you a job. He employs all kinds of people. He's generous that way."

Franz shrugged. He still had his sovereigns.

"A job is the last thing I need at the moment."

When they had finished eating, Franz showed Ariadne around the square. He managed to steer her away from the corner of the building, which still bothered him. They stood awhile by the giant nude in the sun. There was not much else to see. He was half-expecting Two Point Seven to walk by, and looked into the desert.

24

After Ariadne had left through the window, Franz went into the desert, not intending to go far. Just as he was getting used to the emptiness, he suddenly saw a man and a woman coming towards him, emerging from nowhere. He gave them a nod as they passed but they did not seem to notice. It was as if they were dreaming. Not long after that he saw a cloud of steam in the sky, which he soon realised came from a locomotive crawling by in the distance with a train of carriages.

He could not decide which was more disconcerting, the overall lack of life or the sudden evidence of it. The silence around him was so complete that he could hear the blood in his own head, and the sound of his feet on the sand was disturbingly loud. A flashing light caught his eye. As he got closer, he saw that it was reflected from an aircraft—a German fighter. The canopy was open. On the ground lay a naked man. He was a boy really, barely in his twenties. He had a bullet hole through his forehead.

Franz did not go closer, he had no desire to learn more. It made him think of his missed meeting with the Führer. He felt a pang of fear. He had been a failure and would pay a price for it. Could they reach him here? He thought it would be a good idea to turn back but the desert kept beckoning. The landscape was becoming more fecund. He noticed ground cover with little white flowers and clumps of tall grasses. This burgeoning vegetation led to a ruined village. A few structures were partially standing, ringed by a stone wall. As he walked along it he came upon a low, wooden door. He pushed it open and stooped to go through. Inside was an overgrown courtyard, or perhaps what was once a garden. He trudged through dense weeds that reached his waist and found two colossal statues of bronze, lying side by side, the Führer and the Duce, both riddled with bullets.

25

"Am I a killer or a healer?"

His conflicting identities troubled Alexis. That morning he had knifed a collaborator as she knelt before him pleading for mercy. Afterwards he had helped an old woman with back pain. Later he would deal with a black marketeer who had catered to the enemy at the expense of everyone else. Killing people had become easy, especially as he was driven by justice and hatred. Healing was much harder but it was gaining an ever greater influence on him, like an infection he could no longer ignore.

He crumbled out the cigarette between his fingers. On the periphery of his vision he saw Ariadne walking ahead of him. Quietly, he quickened his pace and got right up behind her before she noticed him. It was too late for her to run.

"It's time to atone for your crimes, Ariadne."

Fear caught at the words in her throat.

"Alexis… you loved me once."

"I did, before I discovered who you really were."

He had loved her passionately once. He had wanted to marry her but she spurned him for another. She had been so flippant about it as though he had no importance. He could remember the pain. He could still feel it. She was still so beautiful.

"I kill people like you."

"Please Alexis."

"Don't beg. It doesn't suit you. I'll tell you what. I'll trade you. A life for a life. No. Two lives. That's what your German lovers do, isn't it? Take ten for every one of theirs who's lost. I'll let you keep your life if you give me two in return."

"What do you mean?"

"You are going to have to kill that new German friend of yours."

"I don't have any German friends. The Germans have left.

You know that."

"Don't lie to me, Ariadne. I know what you've been up to."

"But he's not German. He's Swiss. He's never hurt a fly."

"And that's why you were speaking German together?"

"They speak German in Switzerland."

He pulled a knife from his belt.

"Don't say I didn't give you a chance."

"No. Please. I'll do it."

"Good. That's better." He slid the knife back.

"First kill the German, then kill Strange. Otherwise I'll be coming for you."

He stood watching as she hurried off towards the town. His emotions were conflicted. She had always had an effect on him. When he thought of the bargain he had forced her to accept, it did not sit well with his conscience, there was a cruelty to it. He must be getting soft. He had a conscience now. It had never been a problem before. The longer he stood with these thoughts, the greater his regret. By the time he left he wished he had never accosted her. It was too late now. She was on her way.

26

As soon as she had escaped from Alexis, Ariadne headed for Franz's hotel. She tried to be as discreet as possible, taking a roundabout route and not appearing too rushed. She glanced over her shoulder often, half-expecting that Alexis would change his mind and come after her. It was unlike him to let her go. He was known for his ruthlessness. She was cornered. One man wanted her to find a German, and another to kill him. Men were always wanting things from her. Why did the relations between the two sexes have to be so difficult? She played men to her advantage and most of them deserved it, but she was not going to betray Franz. Of all the men she had come across in the last few years he was the most innocent. She still intended to take him up to Strange's house. There was no harm in that. He could always refuse the assignment. Either way, she would have done her job. But kill him? Never. She wasn't going to kill anyone. By agreeing to what Alexis wanted she had bought herself some time, but not much. She would have to find a way around him. It would be be difficult and dangerous.

She came to his window. When she had left the last time, she had placed a rock below it. She stepped up on it and was able to to pull herself in. Franz was lying on the bed, staring at the ceiling.

"Franz."

She climbed up next to him and put her head on his chest. He was in a pensive mood.

"I went into the desert."

"And?"

"The war has reached here too."

She had to find a way to get him to Strange. He had not shown any interest and a job offer had not swayed him. Her fear of indebtedness prevented her from just asking for a favour.

She ran her fingers down his cheek.

"I think I might be pregnant."

"You're what?"

"I said I might be pregnant."

"Who's the father?"

"Who do you think?"

He lay in silence. It seemed too soon. He had never considered becoming a father. That was something other men did. It was not the best time for it either.

"Aren't you going to say something?"

His thoughts had drifted back to the plane in the desert. It gave him a chill. He wasn't in the mood to talk. She seemed relentless.

"Well, what are you going to do?"

She took her fingers from his cheek and rested her head on her arm.

"I think we should go to America and make a new life together."

It was an appealing idea. New York seemed like paradise with its skyscrapers and jazz music. He could be a father. He could be a good one. He would be more present than his own. He certainly did not want to go back to Germany. The Führer's film nauseated him. Directors were often that way. They had an inflated regard for their own importance and weren't concerned for other people.

"How are we going to get there, with things the way they are?"

"We'll need help, Franz. And who better to ask than the man I work for? He has connections everywhere and he likes me. What have we got to lose?"

27

Strange was wearing plus fours and a white shirt with no tie. It was hot. Ariadne stood on the threshold with a handsome young man. Strange was in an affable mood. Things were going his way, as they rightly should.

"Could I offer you some chilled wine perhaps?"

He took some glasses and a bottle from the ice box and led them inside. They sat down on the sofa, opposite his desk. Ariadne introduced Franz and came straight to the point with their request. Franz assumed that Ariadne dispensed with small talk because Strange was the kind of man who liked directness. He was right. Strange did not like meandering, unless it was of his own design.

"You force a paradox on me. If I were to help you in this way, I would lose you."

He downed his glass and poured another. Franz sat quietly sipping. The situation made him feel self-conscious. Strange was a tall man, slender for his age with a heavy jowl and a controlling personality.

"It doesn't have to mean a total separation. I might continue to be of some use to you in America."

He smiled. "True. As a matter of fact, I might be in a position to help you. When do you wish to leave?"

"As soon as possible."

"Ah yes… the impatience of youth." He looked at Franz.

"Perhaps you could do me a small favour in return. I have a package which I need taken up to the German zone. Probably best to go the long way, by sea."

He tapped the bundle before him, wrapped in oilskin and twine.

"If you leave at night you will be back the next morning. Not too difficult. Ariadne here will take care of the arrangements and I will cover your expenses. What do you say?"

"What's in it?"

Strange laughed. "Are you worried about legality? So strait-laced, you Germans. As if legality counts for much these days. If it makes you feel any better, it's a fragment of Mjölnir."

"Mjölnir?"

"You are not familiar with Norse mythology? I thought all Germans were raised on the stuff. Mjölnir, my dear boy, was the hammer swung by Thor."

None of this made much sense to Franz.

"What do I do with it, once I get to the German zone?"

"You will be approached by a man who will ask you to light his cigarette. You will comply and enquire after his aunt. He will tell you that her health is improving and will request the medication you have brought for her. At that point you will hand over the package and your job will be done. Return here and I'll see about getting you both on a ship for the United States. So, what do you think? Will you do it?"

Franz leant back on the sofa and considered the proposition. It seemed straightforward enough. An overnight trip. No more dangerous than driving a coffin to France. If it helped them escape to America, it might be worth the risk.

"I will."

"Very good. You will have to go soon though, while the German zone is still German. Tonight in fact. Now take it, and don't open it for any reason."

He slid the package over the desk.

28

SECRET

S/Ldr D. Noyes
Advanced Intelligence Section,
M.A.A.F. Crete

10th April, 1945

Dear Gilbert,

I have been busy in the last few days and find that in consequence there are one or two matters which have not been attended to. Firstly, the A.D.I.K. Report No. 231 is returned herewith as requested. Many thanks. Secondly, our letters crossed and I received all the details about the mention, afraid however, after some of the people we have seen earn it, that its value is not a little inflated!

The watches arrived safely. I have not yet forwarded Hugh's to him, however. Again many thanks. As for the FuG 16z sets, I expect Jennings has spoken to you about them by now. I don't know how many W/Cdr Morgan wants, but the remainder should be sent to A.I.2(g) via W/Cdr Colrick. The same applies to the RV 12P 2000 valves. Give W/C Morgan as many as he requires of this type (but not the others) and have the rest sent to A.I.2(g). For your information the types LS 50 and LS 180 are particularly sought after in England for keeping all our Wurzburgs on the air; they fairly eat them up and replacements are very difficult to get. The one without the marking looks to me like an LD 2, LD 3 etc. There are so many new V.H.F. types these days.

Enclosed is one roll of 35 mm. film which was exposed some time ago and needs developing. Except for the middle part dealing with the Giant Wurzburg at Pancola, it is unofficial and is to be regarded as a set of trial exposures made upon the acquisition of my new 35 mm camera (with Zeiss f2 lens!) Hence a certain amount of curiosity to see the results.

I too made the ascent of Vesuvio, way back in 1938 while I was yet young. Did it in the middle of the night so as to arrive about an hour before dawn and walked all the way from the main line to Naples at the bottom. Took about 5 hours I believe and we found two boys boxing in the shed halfway up at 0300 hrs in the morning, a thing that I have thought about very often but have never been able to explain.

Yours sincerely,
Daniel

What is this I hear about Goldie? After all the fun he has had. Shilltowe has now written to me saying he wants to go back after all. It is beyond me.

29

Technical Intelligence Section,
Headquarters
Mediterranean Allied Air Forces.

17 April 1945

Dear Daniel,

Many thanks for your letter of April 10th which I found on my return from Oran and Algiers, more about this trip later. I rather agree with your remarks about 'mention'. I am glad the watches arrived safely, I'm sorry I could not bring them myself.

I am dealing with the FuG 16z's and wireless valves as you request, also with the 35m/m roll of film you have sent.

Regarding my trip to North Africa, I am forwarding reports etc. on this to Shilltowe. The aircraft was a JU 88 T-1 with modified nose and no bola which has made a good belly landing having been forced down without a shot being fired from over 20,000 ft. The aircraft was moderately intact. Wireless was normal FuG 10P, EZ 6, Peilgerät 6, 34 spot switch-box, in fact same wireless installation as JU 88 D-1, but with the addition of the FuG 101A.

I managed to borrow a 5 ton crane from the Americans to get the aircraft lifted so that I could see the real item of interest, the GM 1 apparatus with, I hope, the basic boosting substance still present in the large container thus enabling us at least to determine what it is. As you will see from the signal, A.M. agrees with my suggestion re sending it to U.K. and incidentally and rather unusually bestows a bouquet as you will note with which I was quite pleased.

Incidentally I had a very near shave as my tentative arrangement re the crane suddenly materialised on the second day necessitating my having to obtain a Fairchild from Com. Flight Algiers to fly the 190 miles to the site of the crash to be there for the arrival of the crane.

We landed all right in the field (cut corn and rather bumpy) but on taking off, slightly uphill doing about 65 mph just airborne, we hit a low brick wall knocking off our starboard wheel. It was amazing we did not go right in. The pilot (a very nice and good youngish sergeant pilot) asked if I wished to land again and I said no, much better to fly the 190 miles back to Algiers when we should have used most of our fuel and assistance of various kinds would be available at Algiers not available in a cornfield! He also asked if I would like to bale out as we should have to do a crash landing at Algiers, and I told him that I thought that he could land the aircraft better than I could land the parachute.

So to cut a long story short on arrival at Algiers having had one and a half hours to decide our plan of descent, we shot the control tower up by passing over low flapping our wings to attract their attention and ditto the blood wagon etc., and then having decided we would land on the runway rather than off it, having strapped ourselves firmly in (he told me I should probably get the hell of a push in the back and therefore to brace my feet against the bulkhead, which I did), he brought her in very well keeping the wing up as long as possible, we then did a 70 yard slide across the runway, broke the propeller and other tyre but we were intact without a bruise. I was very glad to be on firm ground again but felt none the worse at all. The airfield had turned out to watch our undignified arrival, however all's well that ends well.

Otherwise I enjoyed the trip, meeting some friends, one of whom, a great friend of mine and the family's, took me round the sights of Algiers. He enjoyed it as much as I did. I went over with A/Cdr Reilly in a special aircraft in which he was returning to Algiers and returned by D.C.3. I had lunch at C.S.D.I.C. Algiers, Nancy Weir asked after you. They are all over here now along with the rest of M.A.A.F. rear. Remember me to Hugh and the others. I return Hugh's film and prints. She looks very charming, the old buzzard!

Goldie returned to Cairo last week. He said he felt definitely older these days and that physically after all he found himself unable to cope with roughing it as in the old days. I am afraid he rather noticed the change from the comforts of Cairo to life in a tent, especially as he said that his leg was troubling him a bit. So that's that and one can do nothing more.

I am forwarding all documents requested to A.M. having just perused them and found some very interesting gen amongst other things on the MB 902 Italian aircraft which you and Shilltowe no doubt saw.

Well no more, the best of luck to you all. I know absolutely nothing about the future, so don't know when or if I shall see you soon. Please show this to Shilly and say that I am writing to him.

Yours sincerely,
Gilbert.

30

Back at the hotel, Ariadne helped Franz ready himself for the trip. She placed a cap on his head and pulled up his collar. He was apprehensive. Now that he was about to set out he was beginning to have doubts about this venture. He stuffed the package into his underwear. She suggested they eat before he left, so they went down to the terrace where they were perturbed to find that all the tables were occupied.

"Where did all these people come from?"

They all looked odd to Franz. There were dwarves and mismatched couples, some strikingly beautiful and others just as striking in their ugliness—all of them strangely dressed. They were not the kind of people he expected to see in this restaurant, which was usually empty. It looked like the circus had come to town. His nerves had affected his appetite and he was not particularly hungry anyway. He had only agreed to come down because he did not know when he would get his next meal.

The Chinese man was at his side.

"You want table you come back fifteen minutes."

They did not want to wait so they went back up to their room, stealing a loaf of bread from the kitchen on the way.

"Ready?"

They lowered themselves from the window and set off. It was pitch dark when they reached the waterfront. There was no moon that night so they had to feel their way blindly. When they got to the moorings, Ariadne told Franz to wait and went on alone. Strange had told her to find the seventh boat. The skipper was a man called Stavros. She took with her the money that Strange had given Franz—three sovereigns, and faded into the dark. Franz stood still, listening to the lapping water and the creaking hulls. His nostrils were filled with the fishy and slightly rotting smell of the harbour. He broke some bread and waited.

Ariadne made her way carefully, counting the dim shapes of the boats as they loomed up. She was glad she was not pregnant. Perhaps it was wrong of her to lie but she needed to motivate him, to bring him back to some kind of reality, even if it was a false one. She had not lied about America though. She had always wanted to go there. She loved the films with their dashing heroes and the sultry, intelligent women who manipulated them. And she wanted to go there with Franz. In the short time they had known each other she had grown very fond of him. She usually kept herself emotionally uninvolved with her lovers. It was easier that way, but somehow Franz was different. It surprised her. She looked up and saw that she had reached the seventh boat, the last one in the line.

"Stavros. Stavros."

A large man came out of the wheelhouse.

"What is it?"

"Lord Strange sent me. He wants you to take a man up to the German zone and bring him back."

"Give me a cigarette."

He was gruff and unfriendly. She gave him one of her English cigarettes, which he drew on a couple of times and threw over the side.

"Let me see your coin."

She held out a sovereign. She could barely make out his face. He wore a cap pulled low.

"Give me two. One for the way out and one for the way back." He held out his big hand and she dropped two sovereigns into it.

"Where is he?"

"Just down the dock."

"Better get him here soon. I'm leaving in ten minutes. If he's not here I'm going without him."

Ariadne wondered what he was up to, going out so late at night.

"Make sure he gets there and back safely please."

"That will cost you one more for security."

He held out his hand again and she gave him the last sovereign. Then he turned away and walked back into the wheelhouse without another word. Ariadne found Franz where she had left him.

"It's all arranged. Let's go."

They made their way back to Stavros' boat. When they arrived, he was on the deck, throwing off the mooring ropes. She put her arms around Franz and squeezed him with all the strength her thin frame could muster.

"Take care and come back safely. It won't be too long and soon we'll be out of here for good."

"Get a move on if you're coming."

She pushed him away gently and Franz stepped onboard.

Stavros indicated a spot on the deck and Franz sat down. The engine was idling gently.

"Sit here and don't interfere with anything. And don't bother trying to make conversation."

Franz didn't understand a word he was saying, but he got the point.

Ariadne watched as the boat slipped out, leaving only the sounds of the slopping swell and fading motor as it disappeared into the night.

31

He stayed in his spot without talking, Stavros was at the helm. They made their way out to sea and turned to hug the coastline. Progress was slow. Franz could make out the dim shape of land in the distance. He had no idea where he was. No one had bothered to tell him, and he had forgotten to ask. He thought about how people took their location for granted, something he had always done himself until recently. Putting his observations together, he suspected that he was on a Greek island but his was a curious case, as he did not seem to be in completely the same place as the other people he met.

It was getting cold and his limbs were stiff. The damp from the sea was pervasive and made his skin feel strange. The boat lights were turned off and it was dark except for a gentle phosphorescence coming off the surface of the water. He began to doze, his discomfort causing him to drift in and out of sleep. As he slipped back into consciousness he saw Stavros standing over him with an iron bar, shouting something at him.

He had no time to respond before the bar came crashing down upon his forehead and then he was in the water. He felt himself get sucked down by the draught of the boat. The shock of the blow and the coldness of the sea delayed the onset of pain. All he was aware of was an excruciating struggle for air. His head rose up above the surface and he breathed in gasps, swallowing brine and coughing. His only thought was to get back on the boat. He saw it near him and flailed to reach it. He thought he had his hands upon it but could not pull himself up. The next thing he knew, he was standing in shallow water holding an old boot. He let it fall and waded ashore, collapsing on the beach. He lay face down for some time, shaking and spluttering. It was not sand he lay upon but black volcanic pebbles, which pressed into his face and then his head started to throb.

He rolled over on to his side and wondered why he was still alive. He saw that he was not alone. There were some children playing at the water's edge and a few adults sitting around. He saw a swimmer in the bay. He checked his groin. The package was still there. He tried to understand what had just happened to him but was unable to think clearly and gave up. He lay back down and looked at the sky. It was daytime.

"Good morning."

Two Point Seven was standing over him.

"What are you doing here?"

"I could ask you the same thing. I've changed my number by the way. You can call me Nine from now on."

Franz explained that he had been on a boat, without giving details as to why. He had been hit over the head and thrown into the sea. When he resurfaced he had clung to the side of the boat, only to discover that it was a shoe.

"Yes, flotsam can be misleading."

Franz was annoyed. He had taken too many knocks and the pain in his head exacerbated his bad mood. He had no time for obscure nonsense.

"You always keep showing up and vanishing without explanation. I wonder if I'm just imagining you."

"It's possible we're all imagining each other. It makes no difference really."

Franz looked back up at the sky. It was mostly clear.

"I've found someone who can help you."

"Help me? How?"

"I found someone who can give you answers."

Nine told Franz about a woman he had met in the mountains. She had the ability to move among different metaphysical zones and could describe the paths between them.

"What's that supposed to mean?"

"You might learn something."

Franz was ambivalent. This just sounded like more of Two

Point Seven's, or Nine's gibberish.

"I'll take you up there to see her."

"And disappear again?"

"Maybe."

32

Alexis had been thinking about Ariadne ever since he had threatened her. He wished he could undo what he had done but it was too late now of course. He had just received word that her German friend was dead, killed by the sea captain Stavros. He had apparently beaten him and thrown him overboard. The body had not washed ashore yet, though it surely would in a matter of days. Still, the German had not been seen since, so it was fair to presume he was dead. Stavros was a loner who did not take orders, and aside from his maritime knowledge was as stupid as a plank. For these reasons he had not been accepted into the close group of partisans who regarded Alexis as their captain. They did use him on occasion when they needed to run someone or something up the coast. They always had to pay for those services though, as Stavros had a particularly mercenary nature. He therefore could not be trusted. This matter was further complicated because the German had been involved in some kind of work for Lord Strange. Though Alexis hated Strange, he had changed his mind about having him killed. He had come to see it as an impulsive desire. For the moment he would be more use alive.

These persistent musings, along with his unassuaged guilt, had brought Alexis to where he was today, lurking in the shadows near Ariadne's house. He hoped to intercept her as she came or went. In this he was lucky, as he soon spotted her on her way home. He waited as she approached and then stepped in front of her just as she was reaching her door. She recoiled in fear.

"Don't worry, Ariadne. I'm not here to hurt you. I came to tell you that I take back what I said the other day. You're free from obligation and you won't be harmed, but I would leave here if I were you."

She relaxed but not completely. "Why the change of heart?"

"Just that—a change of heart. There's something else though. I just got a report. Your German friend was killed the other day. I'm sorry."

Her face bunched up momentarily, then quickly became impassive.

"How?"

"I don't know the details. Just something I heard, but reliable enough."

There was obviously nothing else Ariadne wished to say. She walked past him and went indoors.

33

How Franz made it to the top of the mountain in his condition was beyond him. Nine helped at times by dragging him up the steeper slopes. They came to a halt by a cracked rock, from which spring water dripped into a pool below.

"*La akvoj de rekalibrigo.*"

"What are you talking about?"

"The waters of recalibration. You must drink before we continue. We are not far now."

He did not need persuading. He was weak, thirsty and aching, and sank to his knees. He drank from cupped hands. The water was exceedingly cold and refreshing. He could feel it working its way through his body. It had no taste but emitted the faint odour of bananas. He drank until he was finally sated and then rolled over on to his back.

"What about you? Aren't you going to drink too?"

"I already did."

"What language were you speaking just then?"

"Esperanto."

"It's funny, I haven't been conscious of language until you spoke those words."

"We should rest here, while the water does its work. Try to sleep for a bit."

Franz soon fell into a dreamless sleep. He awoke feeling invigorated, his pain much diminished. Nine was sitting next to him, his arms wrapped around his legs. He had never seen Nine this way before. His head, shaven when they had first met, was now covered with thick white blond hair. The skin was tight on his face and his eyes were green. He exuded a glowing pallor.

"I see you are ready. Let's go."

They walked a further five kilometres uphill. Since he had drunk the water, it was much easier going for Franz. He even had a sensation of euphoria. There was a hollow at the top of the mountain, a large basin ringed by coniferous trees and they walked down into it. They followed a stream until they came upon a woman perched on a stool, surrounded by large boulders. She wore a white dress. Nine stepped forward.

"*Saluton. Mia amiko vin bezonas.*"

She glanced at Franz. "*Kion vi havas por mi?*"

Nine translated.

"You must give her something."

Franz did not know what he had to give. He certainly was not going to part with Strange's package, still firmly ensconced in his underwear. There was his gun. He had strapped it to his leg before leaving the hotel and it had managed to survive the ocean. But he wasn't going to give her that either. He fished around in his pocket and found a sovereign. She took it and put it into a linen bag at her side. She seemed satisfied.

"*Nun, vorprenu viajn vestojn.*"

"She says to take off your clothes."

"What?"

"Just do what she says. She can't help you otherwise. You don't have to be a prude. I don't give a damn what you look like naked and I doubt she does either."

So Franz undressed, folding his clothes as he went. He turned away as he pulled down his underpants, discreetly hiding the package in the stack of clothes, then he turned to face her. It felt quite refreshing, standing there naked. She looked him up and down and beckoned him to come closer.

"*Venu. Masturbu en mia buŝo.*"

"She wants you to masturbate in her mouth."

"You're not serious?"

"I'm not but she is."

"I'm not sure I want to do that."

The woman seemed to understand him. She lifted her dress above her hips and parted her legs. Franz did as he was told.

She took the tip of his penis in her mouth. It didn't take long. At one point he looked down on her and saw that she was very old—in her nineties perhaps. Then she resumed her previous age. He stood back. She swilled the semen around, made a face and spat it on the ground. Then she rinsed herself with a handful of water from the stream and sat back on the stool. She looked at him for a few minutes in silence, and then started to speak in a soft monotonous voice.

"*La stultulo ne scias kie li estas,*
nek kien li iros, nek kie li estis.
Nescio de direkto inspiras libereco el loko.
La malsaĝulo kiu posedas ĉi tion liberon
liberigos la urbon de padoj implikaĵaj
sed falos ĉe la manoj de amantino
kiu ne rekonas lin."

After this utterance, she sat still and acted as if they were not there. She said nothing more. Franz had completely forgotten that Nine had been standing at his side the whole time. He struggled with his clothes.

"Would you mind telling me what she said?"

Nine looked up from a reverie.

"*The fool knows not where he is,*
nor where he will go, nor where he has been.
Ignorance of direction inspires freedom from place.
The unwise one who possesses this freedom
will rid the city of entangled paths
but will fall at the hands of a lover
who does not recognize him."

"I don't really understand what it means."

"It doesn't have a specific meaning. It's more about an awareness of change. You could think of it as a kind of motion."

They began to make their way back as they talked.

"I assume you've had a consultation. Did you have to strip and commit a sex act too?"

"It's different for everyone. It's hardly worth talking about. You just have to absorb it. Not just the words but the whole experience. You might be surprised at what happens."

"She seemed to be implying that I am some kind of idiotic civil engineer who will be murdered by his lover. Is that my fate?"

"Fate and destiny are things that one burrows out and follows at the same time."

They were reaching the top of the basin. Nine had gone. Franz was on his own again.

34

On his way down the mountain, he ran into five armed men on their way up. He greeted them to hide his nervousness. They were not fooled.

"Look who have here. The German spy, back from the dead." A rifle butt crashed into his chest and then again into his stomach.

He doubled over and they quickly bound his hands. They found his gun within a minute. Then they spun him around and pushed him ahead of them back up the mountain. They took him to a shack on the side of a gorge. They forced him to his knees.

"We've brought you a gift."

Alexis came to the door, which was just a curtain. He swept it aside and Franz could see the earthen floor within.

"So, the dead German..."

He pulled Franz to his feet again and roughly placed a hand on his shoulder.

"Good job. Just a few questions and a long walk. I'll be back soon."

He winked. The others grinned and set about examining the Luger as Alexis pushed him away from the camp.

After they had gone a safe distance they stopped and Alexis cut Franz's bonds with his knife.

"You're hurt. Sit down."

He did as he was told. Alexis went behind him and, placing both hands on his head, gently probed. He had a light touch for such a fierce man.

"You've got a hard head. You were lucky, there's no fracture. Do you feel faint or sick?"

Franz nodded. It hurt.

"Concussion perhaps. We'll have to be careful."

He ran his hands over Franz's head and down to the nape of his neck, where he let them rest, pressing upwards into the skull with his thumbs.

"Does that feel any better?"

"A bit. Thank you."

"Listen. I'm going to take you somewhere and hide you. Your life isn't worth shit around here."

"I don't understand."

"Don't even try."

Alexis had no idea what he was going to do with Franz. His life had become very complicated. He still had an image to maintain, though he did not know how much longer he could keep it up. He had managed to ensure that his last few victims were not present when he had visited them. The unexpected arrival of this German was difficult. It would have been much easier if he had died at sea. He had to act fast. He came to a lightning decision. He would take him to that priest in the village church.

He carefully helped Franz up and they continued on their journey. The ground was rough and he could barely stand, so Alexis supported him with one arm. It took them over an hour to reach the church. Alexis banged on the door. He never liked to wait at an entrance, it always irritated him. He was also concerned that they would be observed. A priest, in black garb with a beard to match, came out. He looked at both of them with displeasure. Though he considered himself a compassionate man, that did not prevent him from despising Alexis and everything he represented. The feeling was mutual. Alexis sneered.

"Good evening, Father."

"What do you want?"

"I've come to call on the beneficence of the Church. I need a favour."

"Who are you to ask me for a favour?"

"I am a sinner. I heard you liked sinners. They give you

something to think about. Anyway, I need you to hide this man for me."

"In this church? Certainly not."

"What would God have to say about that?"

"You don't know anything about God."

"That's true but let me put it another way. Do as I ask or I will shoot you."

"It's not right."

"If you don't hide him, he'll be killed. Christians don't sanction murder, do they? It will only be for a few days until I work out something else."

"What am I to feed him?"

"Don't cry poor. You'll find something. You always do. It doesn't exactly look as if you are starving.

"I suppose this man's a German, is he?"

"What of it? A man is a man."

"Something has come over you, Alexis."

"Well, will you do it?"

"I suppose so but only for a few days."

The priest extended his hand.

"Don't think I'm going to kiss your hand. There's only so far I'll go. And Father..."

"What now?"

"Thank you."

Alexis left Franz with the priest and took off. When he was out of sight, they heard two gunshots echo through the mountains.

35

It was Sunday and although they were in Crete, they still experienced a hebdomadal malaise—the affliction of an English upbringing. Sunday was a day of stasis and Noyes, who never liked to be idle, was studying his map. They had not received any new intelligence for days. Aside from a few interrogations Purvis performed for the army, there was nothing much for them to do. They knew they would soon be posted again, probably back to Italy, though Purvis was due some leave. Noyes looked up from his map.

"Why don't we go up to Fodele? It's not far."

"What's up there?"

"It's said to be the birthplace of El Greco. We could look around and we might find something interesting. It's only about fifteen miles from here. We could hop in the car and make a day of it. Something to do."

Noyes was a great admirer of the painter El Greco. The elongated figures appealed to him. It seemed an opportunity not worth missing. He always kept his eyes open for culture in the places the war took him. It was a way to affirm life amidst all the horror. Purvis was game. He had nothing else planned, so they took their maps and set out from Mrs. Zombanakis' house.

Fifteen miles did not sound far but once they had left the town the road worsened and when they reached the mountains it became impassable. Fifteen miles might just as well have been one hundred and fifty. They got out of the Jeep and Noyes spread out the map on the bonnet. As they were searching for a way to Fodele on foot, three men appeared leading a donkey. The men were very friendly when they realised they had come upon British officers. One of them spoke English and Noyes asked him for directions.

"That's where we are headed. Come along with us. You can

take turns riding the donkey."

It was an arduous trek through harshly beautiful country and conversation soon dwindled to an occasional curse at the beast. The scent of pine was strong as they followed paths down towards the sea. There was no sign of modernity and the journey was timeless and hypnotic. Noyes was astride the donkey as they finally arrived in Fodele. It made him think of Palm Sunday. He swung a leg and slipped off the animal's back. A crowd was gathering. A girl stepped forward and offered them segments of orange from a tray. Soon after that, a man appeared with a bottle and a glass.

"Welcome to our village. Let's drink to King George."

He poured the glass full and handed it to Noyes, who emptied it in one draught. It had a fiery, acrid taste, pleasantly unpleasant. His eyes watered and he suppressed a cough. He returned the glass and Purvis was next, followed by the man with the bottle and then everyone else. More flasks were brought and the whole process was repeated several times. They were invited to eat at someone's house and were seated at a table outside with ten others. There were oranges again, along with a plate of hard boiled eggs and a little cheese. There was one fork to share among the twelve. It was passed around and they took turns to eat morsels. There were frequent toasts from a single glass.

Both Purvis and Noyes felt uneasy at consuming this food, as the villagers obviously had so little but they would be insulting their hosts if they refused, so they ate sparingly. Noyes checked his watch often, the afternoon was floating by. When it became apparent that the meal was over, they thought they would be on their way but then they were led to another house and the whole scenario was re-enacted.

The owner of this house was the mayor of the village and the food was more plentiful. This time it included a plate of grilled chicken. There was bread and a coarse wine to drink, still from a shared glass. Their host was an older man who had spent his youth in America, where he had owned a restaurant. He had retired to Greece with a sizeable amount of money which the war had whittled away. He spoke fluent English. The conversation flowed through him, as he translated for the others, between mouthfuls. After a lengthy stream of praise for the King, Lloyd George, Mr. Churchill and themselves, Noyes was able to broach the subject of El Greco. Their host seemed pleased.

"You mean Domenikos Theotokópoulos. Yes, he was born here in this village and painted here until he left for Venice. This island was owned by Venice in those days."

There was much laughter and more drinking. Noyes was fully aware of El Greco's biography but he did not interrupt. He listened with a rapt expression, taking a bite from the fork when it came his way.

"We are proud of Domenikos here. He was the only son of our village to amount to anything and that was four hundred years ago."

Noyes emitted a shallow cough and asked if the village was in possession of any artefacts from the great man.

"Sure we are. They are in the church. Go and see the priest. He'll show you."

It was arranged that when they had finished their feast, a boy would take them up and introduce them to the priest. Purvis and Noyes were silently relieved. They were both a little tipsy. The thought of a third meal as honoured guests was not appealing. Acting as emissaries of H.M. Government and of all the Allied Powers was becoming a burden. A quick visit to the church would be the perfect exit. It was certainly much easier to arrive in this village than to leave it. Eventually a boy was summoned and the chairs pushed back. Within ten minutes they were knocking on the church door. Purvis suspected that the priest had been informed of their visit in advance, and even perhaps that their visit to the church had been pre-arranged. As an intelligence officer with a C.S.D.I.C. rating, he had a nose for such things.

"Welcome friends."

The priest spoke English.

"Come in please."

"We gather you may have some things of interest regarding El Greco."

"I do. In the church. Feel free to look."

The paintings were displayed on the interior walls and soon revealed themselves to be poorly executed copies of the master's work. Nothing of interest here. They just had to politely extricate themselves and be on their way. They proffered their thanks and their excuses. On the point of departure Purvis sensed that the priest had something he wanted to tell them.

"Is there anything else, Father?"

"Well actually, yes, there is one thing. It's a sensitive matter."

"How can we help?"

"I'm holding a German prisoner and I think he might be better off in your hands."

"I see. And how did you come by this prisoner?"

"He was forced upon me by the partisans."

"Let's have a look then."

The priest led them down a narrow staircase, his robe rustling. At the bottom he pulled out a key and unlocked a door. It took a moment for their eyes to get used to the darkness. A man was lying on the floor.

"*Aufstehen Sie*!"

The man got up unsteadily and they led him back up the stairs. He blinked as they emerged into the light. He looked to be in bad shape—emaciated, filthy, with an ugly head wound.

"Doesn't look like you've been feeding this chap."

"I've done my best but food is scarce."

They did not admonish him further. There was nothing to be gained by it. As they left the building, a man was waiting for them outside. He was armed and obviously a partisan. The priest introduced him.

"This is Alexis. He's a communist. He will guide you back to your vehicle."

They thanked the priest and followed as Alexis led them down from the church. He turned to avoid the village.

"It's a good thing you're taking this spy. He'll be more use to you than to us."

Noyes did not answer. He was busy supporting the stumbling prisoner. It seemed odd to him that the priest had made a point of telling them that their guide was a communist. He did not like communists. It was a dislike that went beyond politics. It was visceral. To him they represented a threat to the order of things. They implied chaos. It was something he had witnessed far too much. He hated the war and longed to return to life as it had been before.

Alexis kept talking. "This war will be over soon. You'll go back to your soft beds in England but here the fighting will continue and I wonder what side you English will take then. We may not be friends much longer."

Noyes never engaged in political discussions while on duty, especially not with the natives. As far as he could discern, the majority of Cretans were Venezelist in their political opinion, which was not surprising since Crete was his birthplace. Though they were a threat and a nuisance, he did not believe the communists would amount to much. Alexis shut his mouth when he saw that the British were not inclined to talk and led them on a circuitous route back to their car. At least he had solved his problem with the German. When they reached the Jeep, Purvis gave him a photograph of Mr. Churchill, which he threw away as soon as he had parted from them.

They found everything exactly as they had left it. They were pleased to see that the tyres were all there. Finally alone, they tried to sober up before the drive back, drinking water from a metal canteen. Although their quest for El Greco had led nowhere, the day had turned out successfully after all.

36

SECRET and PERSONAL

Party 'A' M.A.A.F.
Field Intelligence Unit
c/o 12th Air Force (rear) APO 650,
U.S. Army.

8th April 1945

S/L. D. Noyes,
c/o Intelligence Section,
R.A.F., A.H.Q. Greece.

Dear Daniel,

Thank you for your letter of 2nd of April from Crete. I am sorry you had to make so many fruitless journeys; Group Captain Stringfellow referred to the fact that M.E. Had made a cock of the arrangements. However, you seem to have been able to achieve some of your other objects satisfactorily.

As you will see I have not left for the U.K. as we are told that the B.F. Operation is to be considered on until definitely cancelled-I may hear some more pretty soon.

We have not had any personal mail for you recently. Some was sent down from M.A.A.F. again from Florence about a week ago as one of them was marked "Please forward as soon as possible". Since then we have only had official mail and a parcel containing a book from England. I received the books you sent from Cairo.

The only other news in the Section is that Swann is going home apparently on compassionate grounds and at the moment nothing is known about a replacement.

If this letter catches you while still at A.H.Q. Greece, Kingsley would like you to enquire whether there is any mail for him or Davies or if any of their kit has been received after the "troubles". S/L Wicks (Org.) may know. Davies has been down at Bari coping with the 15th Air Force's loot, and is arranging for its despatch to England.

Yours,
Shilltowe

37

TOP SECRET

S/Ldr. D. Noyes
Field Intelligence Unit M.A.A.F.
Crete,

18th April, 1945.

Wing Commander Shilltowe
Party 'A'. M.A.A.F. Field Intelligence Uni
c/o 12th Air Force (rear)
APO 650, U.S. Army.

Dear Shilltowe,

Thank you for your letter of April 8. As we had anticipated, the investigation we carried out on Crete was not productive for the parts visited had been evacuated some six months earlier and the combined effects of the weather and looting by the local inhabitants over the intervening period considerably reduced the initially small total of available intelligence. We found less than fifty aircraft on the island, mostly Ju 88s, of which about half were on the four airfields in allied hands, Iraklion, Rethimnon, Castelli and Timbakion, and the remainder in a scrap dump on the docks at Iraklion. The smaller landing strips had been ploughed up for cultivation or had become overgrown and were devoid of aircraft remains. The seven radar sites at Akr. Khersonisos, Ziros, Ierapetra, Eleounda, Akr. Trahili, Palaiokhora and Mouros had been carefully evacuated and nothing was found beyond occasional traces of coast-watcher and Wassermann L installations.

If from the above description our visit may seem to have been ineffective, it must be remembered that the people of many of the more outlying villages had seen no allied troops since the recapture of Crete after the abandonment of the eastern, central and southern parts by the Germans last September. To them the visit had great propaganda value and I feel that much good was accomplished by the direct liaison in the civilian population which was not so much a matter of choice as of necessity. The approaches to the radar sites were invariably through the remotest and wildest parts of the country where first-hand knowledge of the conditions of life on this rugged island were inevitably forced upon one.

On Sunday last, we were engaged in such a propaganda and liaison mission in the village of Fodele. We were treated to great hospitality by the local people who we found to be very enthusiastic about the King, Mr. Churchill and indeed the entire British nation. These people, as in the other villages that were visited, have had to lead a self-supporting existence over the last few years. Cut off from all imports of wheat, rice, sugar, coal and timber from the outside world and very often with only the most slender means of communication between themselves, the standard of living has sunk to a dreadfully low level rendered even worse by the wholesale theft of food on the part of the German and Italian troops. Although originally any supplies taken by the army of occupation were to be replaced in kind, this arrangement appears to have lapsed, inflicting great hardship on the peasant people who had thus a double burden to bear.

In Fodele we discovered a German P/W being held in a lightless hypogeum beneath the local church. The man had apparently been captured by the partisans in the area. The prisoner was handed into our care by the village priest and was found to be wounded and in a state of malnourishment. He has not yet been put through the normal channels and is currently being held at our billet for the exigencies of interrogation.

An initial interview, conducted by F/Lt Purvis yielded no fruitful intelligence. Although it is safe to say that the man cannot be considered an air prisoner. He claims to be a civilian but how he came to be on the island and what he was doing there has yet to be discovered. Incidentally, he speaks fluent English.

However, a very curious object was found on his person, for which he is unable or unwilling to provide an explanation. I have examined it and must confess that I have never before come across anything like it. Without definitive knowledge, I suspect that it is a very technically advanced electronic component the likes of which we have not seen or even knew existed. I believe that this object, no larger than one's thumbnail, may contain vast amounts of circuitry. If I am correct and this technology has been acquired by the enemy, then we have a very serious problem on our hands indeed. It is therefore essential that it be shipped to the War Office in England as soon as possible. Please advise.

Hollis was here on a brief stop-over and delivered two watches from Gilbert for me and Hugh. Seeing as I don't know Hugh's whereabouts these days I was wondering if you might forward his to him. Many thanks. I hear that Goldie has finally returned to Cairo. What can one say about that?

Sincerely DN
Squadron Leader

38

Franz had been locked in the attic room of Mrs. Zombanakis' house. The building was not exactly secure but there was no egress to the roof, so if he attempted escape he would have to pass Noyes' and Purvis' rooms and then get by Mrs Zombanakis herself, who was always home and had no great love for Germans. Purvis had cleaned him up and dressed his wound on the night they returned from Fodele. The next morning they had woken him and given him a British Flight Lieutenant's uniform to wear. It was their custom when treating with English-speaking prisoners—a ploy to erode their sense of identity. They had discovered the package he was carrying when they made him strip naked. Purvis had begun the interrogation by asking the usual preliminary questions—name, number, rank, unit and so forth. When he told them that he was not in the military, things took a menacing turn.

"If you are not a member of the armed forces you are not eligible for prisoner of war status and I would have to consider you a spy. In that case you would have the option of telling us what you know and working with us, or facing the hangman's noose. Your choice."

All this time they had kept Franz standing in the centre of the room while Purvis paced around nonchalantly smoking a cigarette and sometimes asking questions from behind him. Franz never knew where he was going to be next and constantly found himself re-buttoning his fly, which kept coming undone as he stood there. This was another of Purvis' erosive techniques. He had enlarged the button holes for that purpose and he was pleased to see it was having some effect. Franz denied that he was a spy. He was a film technician, no more than that.

"Then tell me your business on the island of Crete."

"I have no business here. I didn't even know this was Crete."

Purvis allowed random time intervals between questions, sometimes delivering a rapid burst and at others lapsing into unexplained silences—all designed to stress the prisoner. He drew on his cigarette and gazed out of the window. It was a bright day and harsh shadows striped the room. They dappled Noyes, who sat at a desk taking notes with his fountain pen on any scrap of paper that came to hand. Paper was hard to come by and he saved the good sheets for his typewritten reports.

"So why don't you know where you are?"

That was a difficult question, verging on philosophy.

"I'm not sure."

"Then tell me how you got here."

"I was driving into France and I found myself here."

"France? A bit off target, don't you think?"

The problem was that he occupied two different worlds and they were firmly placed in one. How was he to explain that and be believed?

"I can't say."

"Where did you drive from?"

"From Berlin."

"And when was this?"

"The summer of 1940. It seems like a long time ago."

"Almost five years, to be precise."

Purvis was annoyed. The interrogation was getting nowhere. Either this man was adroitly feigning a mental condition, or he was truly incapacitated. He could not tell yet. The puzzle intrigued him but he felt he was losing his grasp.

"You say you are a film technician."

"Yes."

"Who employs you?"

"Back in Germany I was working for UFA. It was a company taken over by the state in 1937 I think."

"So you work for the Nazi Government."

"Just about every film production company is now government-controlled. That doesn't make me a spy."

"And what did your work entail?"

"Dressing sets, handling vehicles, animals and so on. Keeping an eye on continuity. That kind of thing."

"Making propaganda?"

"I was just doing my job."

Purvis had walked over to the desk. He turned back towards Franz with a small object between thumb and index finger.

"What is this?"

Franz looked. It was a small black rectangle with eight metal pins extending from it.

"I don't know. I've never seen it before."

"And yet you were carrying it in your underwear."

Franz explained that he had received it already wrapped and had been told not to open it. He had been taken on as a courier in exchange for passage to America.

"Where were you to take it?"

"To the German zone on this island."

"So, you don't know where you are, but you are aware of the German zone."

"I'd never heard of the German zone until he told me."

"Who told you?"

"The man who gave me this thing. I didn't know him. It was the first time we had met."

"What do you think it is?"

"I already told you. I don't know."

"And the man who gave it to you?"

"Strange."

"Is that an adjective or a proper noun?"

"It's a name. A person. An Englishman I think."

"A member of the armed forces?"

"I doubt it. He seems too old. I think he is an archaeologist, or something.

"Did he tell you he was English."

"No. I just assumed he was."

"Did you converse in English?"

"I'm not sure. I don't know what language I'm speaking these days."

"And how did you meet this man? Who introduced you?"

"No one introduced us. He came across me in the harbour. We started talking and he invited me to his house. That's when he made his offer."

"Did he tell you what you would be carrying?"

"He said it was a fragment of Thor's hammer."

"What did he mean by that?"

"I have no idea."

"Let's try again. Why Thor's hammer? A codename is it?"

"I already told you. I don't know."

"And who were you supposed to to deliver it to?"

"I don't know."

Purvis sat down. He was either closing in on a spy ring, or else he was completely lost. He needed time to mull it over and therefore decided to halt the interrogation. He would resume later. He led Franz back up the stairs and locked him in the attic.

Upon his return he asked Noyes his opinion.

"Well, not much useful gen, but this thing..." He held up the object, "this is a different story. It almost speaks for itself."

"What do you think it is?"

"Without making an extensive examination it's hard to be certain but I think it's an electronic component, so advanced that it may render our current technology obsolete. Something like this could dispense with the need for valves. We've got to get it to London as soon as possible. You should haul that chap over the coals. He must know more than he's letting on."

Purvis agreed, though he thought a softer approach might yield better results. They would take him out for a night on the town, give him dinner and get him drunk. They would speak

English together as old friends. Afterwards they would let him spend the night with a woman. A little pillow talk might do the trick. It had worked before and he knew a girl who would fit the bill very nicely.

Noyes was not convinced. "Don't you think he might try to escape?"

It was a reasonable concern. They could find themselves in trouble, seeing as how they had deviated from protocol with this prisoner but Purvis was confident.

"Where's he going to go? A lone discombobulated German on this part of the island, even if he does speak English? I don't think he'd last long without our protection."

39

He had no intention of trying to escape. He was much better off with the British than with the partisans. If he could make it back to the hotel he would be safe but the risks of getting there were great and he did not yet feel physically capable. He would stay put.

Franz was sitting on his narrow bed with his face in his hands. He had been sitting in that position since Purvis brought him back upstairs. What could he say to convince them of his innocence? He could not expect them to believe his story, he hardly believed it himself. He had told the truth as best he could, with some omissions. He didn't want to implicate Ariadne. No doubt they would question him some more. He would not mention his personal meetings with the Führer, Himmler and Goebbels either. That was bound to create the wrong impression. He also would not tell them about the hotel. He wanted to keep it his own secret refuge. He could play the madman, since he suspected that it was something Purvis was considering, but if he laid it on too thick he would see through it. That damned object he was carrying would condemn him if nothing else did.

He thought about what that strange woman had told him on the mountain. She had called him a fool. Yes, he was a fool, probably in more ways than he could imagine. Perhaps it was his fate. Nine had described fate almost as a prison one created for oneself. He always took on the role of teacher in their relationship. It was annoying. He had saved Nine's life and this was his reward. There was something smug about Nine, who patronised him as if he was an idiot—a fool… but then the woman had seemed to suggest there was some kind of honourable quality to being a fool.

He had obviously been betrayed. There were only three people who came to mind—Strange, Ariadne and the sailor, either working alone or in cahoots. Why would Strange take him on as a courier only to have him killed a few hours later? And why would Ariadne want him dead when she seemed so fond of him? That left the sailor, who had not even tried to rob him. Was he paid or was he acting alone on some psychopathic whim?

His brain was foggy. It was hard to make sense of the situation. He ran his fingers across the bandage on his head. His wound was still painful but it was healing. He supposed he should consider himself lucky.

Across from his bed there was an old wood stove against the wall that he gazed at through his hands. It did not look as if it had been used for a long time. As he stared at it he imagined that he was hearing music coming from within. He listened for a while and then went over to it and opened the door. He was not dreaming. Music was definitely emanating from the wood stove. The music of bagpipes.

40

Purvis had been asked to conduct an interrogation by Major Randel, who would be arriving in town that afternoon along with a prisoner. He had sent a message to Dimitra, via a street urchin and was going to meet her first. He left Mrs Zombanakis' house and immediately crossed the street to avoid a group of bagpipers on the corner. He hated the sound of bagpipes. Their infernal caterwauling was a pernicious reminder of the fragile nature of civilization. These were the Greek variety but they led him to wonder how the King was able to tolerate pipers outside his window at Balmoral when he took luncheon. Perhaps he did so for the sake of tradition, as an act of generosity to Scotsmen. The thought amused him and made him laugh. He was in an optimistic mood. It was a fine day and he had a concrete problem to solve. He was going to enlist the services of Dimitra. He would break that Hun if it took her all night.

They met in one of their usual spots close to the docks. He explained the gist of the situation and what was required of her. Ariadne was quietly ambivalent although she had done worse, and agreed to do as he asked. She looked drawn.

"Are you unwell?"

"Just tired."

Purvis needed to get her to probe for information regarding the component without revealing its importance. Noyes had nicknamed it 'The Arachnid' because it had eight legs. Noyes was absolutely beside himself and in a curious state of frustrated elation. He considered it the most important find of the war. He wanted to cut into the thing and examine it but he knew he shouldn't. He did not have the right equipment and would only damage it. At one point he was all for dashing off and looting a municipal science building or hospital to acquire a microscope as if such things existed where they were. Noyes had a predilection for top notch scientific instruments and had collected quite a few in Italy, none of which were with him at present except for his typewriter. He had always wanted a typewriter but had never been able to afford one. It was a necessity, so one day while driving through a town he had suddenly pulled over and entered an office building. Moments later he emerged with a very high-quality machine, right past two Italians arguing about something in the foyer. He was very pleased with that acquisition and would not be parted from it. He used it for all his reports.

"We found a tiny object on him. See if you can find out what he knows about it."

"I'll do what I can."

He patted her knee and she flinched inwardly. He pulled a small pistol from his pocket and gave it to her.

"If he tries to run, shoot him. Just please don't kill him. Do you know how to use this thing?"

"I can manage."

"Splendid."

They let Franz stew alone in his room with no food for the rest of the afternoon, to soften him up for the night's business. Several hours after sundown Purvis climbed the stairs and banged on the door.

"You decent?"

Without waiting for a response, he unlocked it and let himself in. Franz was lying on the bed.

"Get yourself up. We're going out for a little R and R."

He had brought up a fresh pair of trousers, this time with un-doctored button holes, and he helped Franz by straightening his uniform and making him look as a British officer should when he goes out on the town. As soon as Franz was presentable they went down to meet Noyes who was waiting by the front door.

41

Despite the privations of war, the Jazz Bar looked quite cheerful when they entered. The candles on every table and the black-out in the windows made for a cosy atmosphere. The orchestra was in full swing. This was just the kind of place Purvis liked. He found it exciting and intimate, full of promise. Noyes considered it brash. He preferred classical music. This was just one of their differences. Franz could not understand why they were taking a prisoner and a potential spy out to a night club. What would it be tomorrow—a trip to the cinema? The British were definitely very strange. Purvis ordered cheese and olives.

"What's your poison Henry? Wine or spirits?"

"Wine I think."

"Good. We'll try some of the hard stuff later."

No sooner had their drinks arrived than a British military man sauntered up. He had a moustache and clean chin. His poise bespoke control. They all rose from their chairs.

"Ah Major Randel, we meet again. You know Noyes of course. Allow me to introduce Flight Lieutenant Henry Rawlins R.A.F. just with us for a few days. Would you care to partake?"

"No thanks. Just on my way out actually." He glanced briefly at Franz.

"Pleasure to meet you."

When the major had left, suspecting nothing, Franz knew he had passed his first test. It was quite exhilarating. They sat down again and started to drink. Purvis was attentive and kept his glass full. Soon Franz began to feel a pleasant warmth in his stomach. This was the best he had felt in days. These British really weren't bad at all. Purvis talked a great deal about sports cars and rugby. Noyes told them of his ascent of Mount Vesuvius and the boys he had found boxing on his way down in the middle of the night, the significance of which he had never been able to fathom. He was more reserved than Purvis and did not seem completely at ease. They both avoided talking about the war. Franz started to describe some of his more salacious adventures with Leni Riefenstahl when Purvis gently admonished him by tapping him on the elbow and telling him to keep it English. Another carafe of wine arrived and glasses were refilled. The place was full of smoke and the music was loud. Everybody looked like criminals. Noyes glanced around him in distaste.

"Look at them all."

"Excuse me?"

"These people who have been spread across the world as a result of the war. They don't bring any form of culture with them. Their minds know only pleasure, invariably associated with the consumption of large quantities of alcohol. It's a terrible thing that in England much more money is spent on beer than on scientific research. If something had been set aside for the defeat of submarines and bombers, our own country and several others might not be in the pitiful condition they are today. People still prefer to cross their bridges when they come to them instead of planning ahead. The result is one continuous muddle. Shall we ever learn?"

Noyes' outburst put a damper on things and there was a lull in the conversation. Franz looked up to see Ariadne making her way across the room towards them. They were all quickly on their feet and Purvis again made the introductions.

"Dimitra. What an unexpected pleasure. May I present Squadron Leader Daniel Noyes R.A.F. and Flight Lieutenant Henry Rawlins R.A.F. He's had a bit of a prang but I think he'll live. Please join us."

He pulled out a chair for her. Franz could not tell if she was surprised to see him for she showed no sign of ever having met him and politely shook his hand before she sat down. He understood and raised his hand to his wound to cover any expression that might have betrayed him. He had no cause to worry, as both Purvis and Noyes had their eyes on Ariadne and he had been forgotten for the moment. Purvis chatted away amiably.

He turned to Franz, "How about we move on from the vino? They have this local liquor here. Made from old grape skins I believe. Quite powerful stuff."

He ordered four rakis. The conversation did not flow easily. Franz had nothing to say. He had too many questions but he could not ask them. Noyes was silently smouldering over the deplorable state of humanity and Ariadne was waiting to see what would happen. That left Purvis, who was trying to be cheerful. He was rescued by the arrival of the rakis and they passed a few minutes on initial sips.

"Good stuff don't you think? Rawlins, why don't you ask Dimitra here for a dance? Don't be frightened. She won't bite."

It seemed like a good opportunity for privacy so Franz followed his suggestion.

"Dimitra, would you do me the honour?"

She accepted and they moved away from the table. He clasped her chastely and directed her close to the orchestra, where they would not be overheard. She felt good in his arms.

"I thought you were dead."

"I did too. Was it you who tried to have me killed?"

"Of course not."

Their ears brushed each other's lips.

"I didn't think so, but someone did. How are you?"

"Happier now that I know you're alive."

"And how is the baby doing?"

"There is no baby, Franz. I'm not pregnant."

"What do you mean?"

"I was late, that's all."

He felt a tinge of disappointment. She seemed to brush it off so casually.

"Well it's probably for the best, considering the world we're living in."

"Yes. There'll be time."

"So who do you think wanted to kill me? Was it Strange?"

She admitted that Strange had told her which boat to use but she couldn't see why he would want to kill him. It had to be Stavros, acting on his own.

It made sense he supposed. Though he still had some suspicions about Strange.

Ariadne looked up at him and spoke softly.

"Listen, we don't have much time. The British think I am working for them. This whole night out is a set-up. They are going to let you spend the night with me so I can extract information from you. They are particularly interested in that thing you were meant to deliver."

"I wish I'd never taken it. It will put a rope around my neck."

"We've got to tell them something."

"But I don't know anything."

"We'll go up to Strange's house tonight and see if we can get some answers. One more thing. Don't run off on me or I'll have to shoot you."

She smiled and ruffled his hair. The orchestra was playing *Cheek to Cheek*.

42

When they returned to the table, Both Purvis and Noyes had already left. Outside in the cool air, Franz felt a little shaky on his feet. He put his arm through Ariadne's.

"What's this Dimitra stuff about? Is Ariadne a false name too?"

"Well what about Henry? It suits you though."

Ariadne was guiding them towards her lodging. Not somewhere she usually took anyone. In fact, she had no intention of reaching it. She was merely checking to see if they were being followed and when it became obvious that they were not, she changed course. They found their way to the base of the hill in the moonlight. Franz was sobering up. As they made their ascent he felt calm, but he had a lurking sense of foreboding. The cypress trees appeared first and then the gateway, sinister in the darkness. Ariadne said she would wait outside and he should go in alone. She told him to be careful.

Strange was still up and in shirtsleeves. He let Franz in with his usual politeness and did not ask why he was visiting so late.

"I see you have joined the R.A.F. since we last met."

Franz looked down at his uniform. He had forgotten he was wearing it. He had decided beforehand that he was going to be firm and aggressive but the comment threw him off.

"I was wondering about the arrangements for my passage to America."

"I don't believe you kept your side of the bargain."

"So you know what happened to me?"

"I know that you didn't make the delivery."

"It's not my fault. There was an attempt on my life."

"That's not my fault either. You knew there were risks."

Strange's veneer of friendliness had fallen away, leaving behind it a steely coldness. Franz felt suddenly exhausted.

"I know why you're here, even if you don't. Sit down."

Franz felt himself slipping back into the sofa.

"What was it I was carrying for you?"

"I told you once. Don't you remember?"

Franz had no resistance left in him. He was not sure what he remembered. He struggled just to stay awake.

"Sleep."

Whether it was because of the alcohol, or the wound, or some hypnotic suggestion, a terrible fatigue was creeping through his body, robbing him of reason. He was teetering on the threshold.

"... got growing again ... I am over by the blood of them ... run by there."

"Sleep."

There were rows of columns stretching into the distance, lit by the moon. He hid behind them as he moved among them. He had a purpose he did not know. As he moved he saw that the columns were a town of shattered buildings. He climbed over piles of rubble in the streets. There were hundreds of people working high up on the walls and on scaffolds. They were painting the stones to make them look older. He came to a barrier across the road, a wrought iron fence. It was the separation of two places that looked the same. He approached it and put his face against the bars. He watched a man coming towards him with a hat and cane. It took a long time for him to emerge from the darkness until eventually they stood facing each other on opposite sides of the fence. Franz saw that it was Strange. They stared at each other for a while and then Strange spoke.

"I will eat your dreams."

As soon as he had uttered these words he was gone. So was the fence and the entire ruined city. All of it was replaced by an endless plain of flagstones. Franz kept going. Occasionally he came across holes in the stones, a palm's width in diameter. They were ringed in iron and spewed white plumes of steam. There was a roaring sound as the vapour was emitted into the night sky. Near one of these holes he saw a man sleeping. Franz looked down at him. It was Strange again, his hat by his side and his cane clasped with both hands on his chest. Then Franz knew what he had come to do. He balled his fists and savagely drove them into Strange's head. His fists unclenched and he tore at the face with his fingers. Within minutes he had ripped away all the flesh and plunged down through the eye sockets into the brain. He got up and walked away, wiping the blood on his shirt. He wandered down corridors with right angled turns and narrow staircases. There was not a curve in sight. With each step he knew that he was becoming more entombed. He could hear a woman calling his name.

"Franz... Franz."

He could not tell from which direction she was calling. He couldn't see anyone. Then the voice became more present.

"Franz. You're naked."

It was Ariadne bending over him as he lay on the sofa.

"Come on. Get dressed. We have to go."

The resonance of the dream stayed with him and it took him a long time to get dressed.

"Where's Strange?"

"I don't know. Come on. Quick."

She helped him with his shoes and led him outside. They ran through the gate, past the trees and made it to the road without looking back.

43

(5/145) Wt. 37906/1498. 200M pads. 12/39. B & S Ltd. 51-8665.
R.A.F. Form 96.
S 575 (Naval)

MESSAGE FORM

Office Serial No.

Call IN and Preface OUT | No. of Groups GR | Office Date Stamp.

TO* RAF HERAKLION

FROM* MAAF | Originator's Number AL 369 | Date | In Reply to Number and Date

REQUEST FOLLOWING BE PASSED
S/LDR NOYES OF TECHNICAL
INTELLIGENCE MAAF. GROUP
CAPTAIN S?RINGFELLOW
PROPOSES BRIEF VISIT HERAKLION
21 APRIL REQUEST S/LDR NOYES
AVAILABLE WITH ARA?NID
(TWO CORRUPT GROUPS)

ESTIMATED TIME OF ARRIVAL
0630 HERAKLION AERODROME
DATE 20/4

This message must be sent AS WRITTEN and may be sent by W/T. Signature | This message must be sent IN CYPHER and may be sent by W/T. Signature | Originator's Instructions.* Degree of Priority.* | Time of Origin.

T.O.R.

T.H.I.

* The Signal Department is responsible that these details are transposed to the appropriate portion of the message form and that all possibility of compromising distinguishing signals, etc., by omitting to remove their signification from the address, etc., is avoided. Before delivery of the message these details are to be re-inserted in P/L.

44

By the time Ariadne brought Franz back to the house as promised, Noyes had already left to meet Group Captain Stringfellow and pass on the Arachnid. Mrs Zombanakis was on her way to church. She gave them a sour look in passing. She did not approve of Germans, or women like Ariadne. Today her dislike was intense as it was a saint's day and their iniquities seemed all the more insulting.

Franz had wanted both of them to run, they could stay in the hotel until they worked something out.

"Why would a free man give himself up as a prisoner?"

"You're not a free man, Franz. The hotel is on the island, isn't it? They'd be sure to find us. Then we'd be in a much worse situation, and the people here don't like Germans. No one would help you."

"Except you."

"Except me."

For a moment Ariadne had thought about fleeing too. But where? Hiding in the mountains with the partisans wasn't an option for either of them.

"Both of us would be safer if you go back. I'll put in a good word for you. Even if you're made a prisoner of war, it's not forever. At least you'll stay alive."

Purvis came down to meet them and had her wait while he locked Franz back in the attic. Then he took her into his room.

"What do you have for me?"

She had been preparing herself for this moment. She started with Franz's arrest by the Gestapo in Berlin and his meeting with Adolf Hitler. She had persuaded Franz that it would be a good idea to give them this, as he had withheld it and it would therefore give the previous evening some credence. She had to look out for herself as well. She told Purvis how he had been ordered to work on a propaganda film and drive to France with another man whose name he did not know or remember. He had insisted to her that this man went by a number. This was just one fact among many that convinced her Franz was mentally confused. She did not think he was lying but that he was suffering from some type of amnesia. She had not been able to determine the cause, although she did not believe it was the result of the wound he had recently received because his capacity for more recent memory seemed to be unaffected. As far as she was concerned, she thought he was telling the truth when he said he did not know where he was or what year it was. At some point he had met, or perhaps been sought out, by a man he called Strange. This man persuaded him to act as a courier in return for assistance with escape to America. He was instructed to take a package to the German zone but had been beaten over the head and thrown into the sea by the man he had hired to take him there. After that he had been captured by the partisans.

"The rest I think you know."

"Did you manage to get information about the package?"

"Not really. He told me he never looked at it until you showed it to him. He doesn't know anything about it beyond being told it was a bit of Thor's hammer—what does that mean anyway? He's very worried that you will condemn him as a spy. I don't think he is, for what it's worth. He just seems to me like a confused and troubled man. There are plenty of those about."

"This man Strange. You haven't met him by any chance, have you?"

"No. I've never heard of him. Not until last night."

Purvis looked disappointed.

"Well that's enough for now. Thank you Dimitra."

Noyes returned several hours later. He had given Stringfellow the Arachnid along with his suspicions, which were redundant as he had already written about them to Shilltowe. He had never met the Group Captain before. He must be new at M.A.A.F. He seemed capable and decent enough. The only firm impression that Noyes had come away with was that he was not well suited to his name, being of short and stocky physique. Though he knew it was for the best, parting with the Arachnid left Noyes feeling depressed. He would gain great kudos if his conjectures turned out to be correct, if it was not snatched away from him. He had firsthand experience of the machinations rampant in the services. Too many times he had been studying important documents when a superior officer from another branch had walked into his room and taken them from him with a mere: "What are you keeping from us now?" How was he to do his work? It had happened with the *Flug*. He had been the first person to discover and comprehend it, only to have it pulled away. He had the same reservations about the Arachnid.

There was a knock on his door and Purvis came in.

"I don't like it. The whole thing is queer. Nothing adds up."

"Didn't you get any gen off the girl?"

"A little. Nothing very helpful. Not much I didn't know already. I'm wondering who this Strange chap is."

"What strange chap?"

"The man he told us about. If there was an English archaeologist around here, you'd think we would have heard of him, wouldn't you?"

They decided the best course of action was to go and see for themselves. They would have Franz introduce them to this man, if he existed, and then they would act accordingly. They would be a little harder on the prisoner. The soft approach had not worked.

Franz was asleep when they burst into the attic.

"Get up!"

He was feeling tired and hungover. Purvis grabbed him roughly and pushed him through the doorway and down the stairs. They clambered into the Jeep outside.

"We're going to visit Mr. Strange."

"Lord Strange."

"So he's a lord now, is he? Do you remember the way?"

Franz nodded. Noyes fired up the engine and they pulled off. Soon his left leg began to dangle. He wished he could taste marmalade.

Before long they reached the hilly road that led up to the villa. On the two occasions he had been there before Franz had walked but now, arriving so quickly by car, he felt somehow cheated. The experience seemed less real.

"This is it."

They parked by the gate and went on foot to the house. The door was ajar.

"Hello?"

There was no answer so they let themselves in. The place was empty. The furniture had gone and the glass in the windows was broken. There was a hole in the roof that had let in the weather.

"This the right place?"

"I think so."

"When did you say you were last here?"

"About a week ago. Maybe longer."

"Well it doesn't look like anyone has been living here for years."

They went from room to room. There was no sign that Strange had ever been there. Franz was full of doubts. He had been certain this was the villa but now he was not so sure. They went into the study and Purvis chuckled.

"Looks like one of our locals left his calling card."

There was a human turd on the floor in the middle of the room.

45

c/o G-2 Air, 13 Corps 26.4.45

Dear Daniel

Gudrun reports that the activity where he has been is highly suggestive and reminiscent.
I think you should ask Major Randel to find out if we are to be involved and if so if we are to return to HQ first. None of us wish to take part in anything without returning to go over our personal kit left behind at HQ, so ample warning is required. We cannot be expected to go straight off on some jaunt in our present state-or can we?
BURN

Yours sincerely
G.R. Shilltowe

46

"Who was the man that accompanied you when you thought you were driving to France?

"I don't know. I'd never met him before. He was taken from a prison camp and I was ordered to kill him. I think he was an artist of some kind."

"What was his name?"

"He never told me. He referred to himself with a number. When we first met it was Two Point Seven. He later changed it to Nine."

"Why were you ordered to kill him?"

"It had something to do with the film the Führer was making."

"What was the point of it?"

"How do I know? It never made sense to me. But in the film business sense isn't necessarily the main motivator. Whim has a lot to do with it. What they call 'vision' in the trade. It was an order. A *Führerbefehl*. Are you allowed to question your superiors?"

This whole story was ridiculous. Purvis liked to think that he had some skill as an interrogator but he was starting to feel like an amateur, a fledgling schoolmaster trying his hand at intelligence work.

"Where did you learn to speak English?"

"From my mother. She was a school teacher. English was her subject."

"Did you kill him?"

"Who?"

"This Nine chap."

"I just told you I didn't kill him."

"So you disobeyed an order."

"I did. Not the first time either."

Franz was beginning to enjoy this conversation, despite the threat that hung over him. To see Purvis so frustrated was entertaining. The beauty of it was that he was telling the truth. He knew his story did not make sense.

"So where is Nine now?"

"I couldn't say. He shows up from time to time unexpectedly. He vanishes, he reappears. To be honest, I've often wondered if he exists only in my own mind."

Purvis had wondered about that too. It was obvious to him that they would get nothing useful from this prisoner, spy or not. He had no technical knowledge. In fact he had no knowledge at all. He was a fool, living in a complete fantasy world. Damaged goods. At least they had the Arachnid.

"What unit did you desert from?"

"I'm a civilian. I told you that already."

He was probably a deserter. A mental case, an amnesiac. That was the most likely explanation. It was time to dispose of this man.

47

TOP SECRET

FIELD INTELLIGENCE UNIT

Instructions for passage to CORSICA from R.A.F. CASTELLI
S/Ldr NOYES
F/Lt PURVIS

You are to report on 30/4/45 at 07.25 hours at CASTELLI for passage to CORSICA by M.A.T.S. Aircraft leaves approx 08.10 hours

100 lbs of kit plus 60 lbs of essential technical equipment may be carried. A certificate for technical equipment is attached

On arrival, report to D.A.F. Detachment (possibly renamed R.A.F. Admin. Group), contacting W/Cdr DALE at FURIANI, map reference QD2559. Then join 2788 Sqdn. R.A.F. Regt. based at FURIANA (QD2560). Bring cameras and film and any further mail for officers and c/r's.

for Air Commodore
Chief Intelligence Officer
Mediterranean Allied Air Forces

48

So much for ample warning. Purvis was furious that his home leave had been cancelled again. They had to depart in two days. It left little time to put their affairs in order. They also had to dispose of their prisoner, which meant driving him out to the Major at Rethimnon, where he could be transported to a camp in Egypt or wherever else they chose to send him. Matters had been made worse when they received a telegram that morning from Shilltowe, informing them that the aircraft carrying Group Captain Stringfellow had been lost over the Aegean and so far not a trace had been found.

Despite his irritation at having to part with the Arachnid, Noyes had been pleased that it would be going to London with a competent officer. He'd previously had some bad experiences shipping back salvaged material to England. A large Wassermann which had left him in pristine condition, arrived some months later fit only for the scrap heap. It had taken considerable effort to salvage that machine, enlisting a crane from the Americans and finding a suitable vessel. After that, he vowed never again to send anything back unaccompanied.

Now the Arachnid was lost forever, and an opportunity for technological advancement gone with it. He felt as if he had nothing left to give but he knew there was no option other than to persevere. For this reason, and as a means of distraction, he told Purvis that he would drive the prisoner out to Rethimnon. He had already settled up with Mrs. Zombanakis who was very happy with the meagre sum he gave her, telling him over and over that the Germans had paid her nothing. He had also purchased some of her husband's clothes, which she still kept in a drawer. Franz was forced to shed his Flight Lieutenant's uniform and be refitted.

Noyes was nervous. He spent some time cleaning his revolver

and checking the ammunition, then he went to fetch Franz and put him in the Jeep. He was not in the mood for conversation. Aside from his dismay about the Arachnid, Noyes was glad to be going back to Italy. He liked the country. He had found a good piano teacher in Naples and intended to pick up the lessons again, if not in Naples then somewhere else. Italy was full of starving maestros.

"Where are you taking me?"

"To Rethimnon. You'll be shipped out to a camp. Probably in Egypt."

Then there was silence. Neither man felt like talking. There was only the sound of the engine. They were on the road, high in the mountains, in the middle of nowhere, when the engine sputtered and died. They cruised to a stop. Noyes got out and opened the bonnet. The problem was a ruptured hose. Not too serious. He got his tools from the back and buried himself in his repair work. On an impulse which had been building for a while, Franz took his chance. While Noyes had his head under the bonnet, he slipped over the side and ran as fast as he could into the wilderness. He did not waste time by looking back.

49

Franz kept running as long as he could. It was early evening, he had come quite some distance from the road and had neither seen nor heard any sign of pursuit. He slowed to a walk and tried to think of a plan. Noyes would no doubt have informed the Major and the army would be out for him. They might send spotter planes and then of course there were the partisans to worry about. He was looking forward to nightfall. It had been a stressful day but wandering in solitude calmed him a little. His clothes were too big and he was not sure exactly where he was. He thought that he needed to go east and was able to find that direction by walking away from the sun which was just beginning to set. Soon it would be too dark to walk and he looked around for a suitable place to pass the night. Tomorrow he would find his way back to the town and then to his hotel. He knew he would be safe there, despite what Ariadne had said. She couldn't grasp how a place could be somewhere and not, at the same time. He didn't understand it either but he had a sense of it. The hotel would protect him with its unreality. Maybe Ariadne would join him there and some day they would reach America.

Ahead of him was a wizened olive tree. He saw a man leaning against it, who looked familiar.

"Nine. Is that you?"

"Not any more. Forty-Five now."

"Tell me, why is it that you randomly appear and disappear?"

"I oscillate between existence and non-existence. But don't assume it is random."

They sat for a few minutes in silence, then Forty-Five reached into his pocket and pulled out a rectangular strip of paper.

"Here's something interesting. Watch this."

He looped it into a ring by holding the narrow edges together then he twisted one edge and rejoined them.

"See? A Möbius strip, a closed Möbius strip, a non-orientable object. It has only one side and one boundary. Two planes have become one. The inside is the outside."

He ran his finger along the plane to illustrate his point.

"You can have two kinds of Möbius strips depending on whether you make a clockwise or anti-clockwise twist but that is splitting Euclidean hairs. They still have the same properties either way. It's a beautiful thing don't you think? You could describe it mathematically as:

$x\ (u,v) = 1 + v/2 \cos u/2 \cos u$

$y\ (u,v) = (1 + v/2 \cos u/2) \sin u\ z\ (u,v) = v/2 \sin u/2$

where $0 \leq 2\,\Pi$ *and*

$-1 \leq v \leq 1$

Or you could think of it more poetically. For example, take that idea of two planes becoming one and apply it to the concept of the self. The boundary between one self and another would be dissolved, so therefore you and I might actually be considered the same person. I said that I oscillated between existence and non existence. If you applied the Möbius strip to that thought, then there could be no oscillation, because existence and non-existence would be the same thing. That would imply that I do not exist. Do you know, the Möbius strip was discovered by a couple of your countrymen? What gets really interesting is when you cut one lengthwise and then cut it again and again. I don't have scissors with me, otherwise I'd show you but you should try it yourself some time."

Franz was fast asleep on the ground.

50

At about 9:30 the next morning Ariadne went to Mrs Zombanakis' house. She had woken up listless without knowing why, until she realised that she wanted to see Franz again. She was worried about him and what the English might do. She liked him more than she should. She tapped on the door. Mrs. Zombanakis, being broad of beam, filled the frame. Ariadne tried to peer over her shoulder into the house.

"I've come to see Flight Lieutenant Purvis."

"He's gone. They are both gone. Gone for good."

Mrs. Zombanakis was intelligent. She understood why Ariadne had come. She hated this girl, so young and beautiful, who trampled all over every shred of decency. All for the sake of her own advancement. She had been carrying on like that for years, while other women toiled and struggled to care for their families. What made it worse was that she had done quite well for herself, better than most. Mrs. Zombanakis was furious. Her little eyes twinkled.

"Where's the prisoner?"

Mrs. Zombanakis ran her hand across her throat with a hissing sound.

"He's gone too. The dark haired one did it. I saw him cleaning his gun, then he took the German away and came back without him."

She paused to study her effect.

"They are busy men these English. They have a war to fight. They don't have time for prisoners."

Ariadne did not know whether to believe her or not. She was a jealous old bitch. The only lover she had was Jesus.

As she stood blocking the doorway, Mrs Zombanakis was having her own angry thoughts.

"She'll go with anyone. She's a whore. I don't want to defile myself by talking to her. Who knows who's watching?"

She slammed the door shut in Ariadne's face.

Ariadne stood for a while, digesting the vitriol. That old hag knew how she felt for Franz. The British must have taken him somewhere. They didn't seem like executioners. But either way, it was unlikely she would see him again. She went back home. These past years had exacted a price. Hope seemed stupid.

51

Soon it would be time to say goodnight to the children. He loved them profoundly, all six of them. Had they been old enough to make their own decisions, they would have agreed with him that death with the Führer was the only honourable course of action. Magda agreed. She had no desire to live in a world where the beacon of National Socialism had been extinguished. She had always been more in love with the Führer, he thought, than with him.

They had been living in this bubble for nine stagnant days. Nine days that seemed eternal. There was nothing much he could do but set the record straight, while waiting for the inevitable.

He thought about the fact that, among all the members of the Party elite, he was the only one who had stayed with the Führer to the end. Only he had possessed the fortitude. The Führer had ordered him to leave and he had refused. It was the only time he had ever disobeyed him. He had made the right decision. It was not that he relished death but he had a choice—to be the architect of his own, or let the Russians do it.

They had heard with dismay of the fates of Mussolini and his mistress. Much better to die with dignity and honour in the privacy of the *Führerbunker*. He had made the arrangements. Magda would give the children sleeping draughts with their evening meal. As soon as they were asleep, she would administer the poison he had provided. After they had assured themselves that the children were safely dead, they would withdraw to their bedchamber and, as soon as he saw Magda bite down on the cyanide capsule, he would shoot her. He would then do the same to himself. He had instructed his adjutant Schwaegermann, to enter the room after he had heard the two shots, and carry their bodies up to the garden for incineration. He would cheat the Russians and they would die martyrs. What mattered to him now was the legacy he would leave behind.

He had no regrets but one. They had not finished their film. It had been a labour of love for both him and the Führer. It had been such an exciting time, a fascinating burst of creativity. He wondered what had ever become of that Leis fellow. When he had never arrived in Paris, he believed that Leis must have betrayed them and deserted. Later, a report had come in about a wrecked vehicle, probably destroyed by the Luftwaffe, which had been discovered in a ditch in Northern France. It was found to contain two charred bodies, too badly burnt and decayed for identification. So perhaps he had remained true after all.

Time was running short. He was aware that Schwaegermann and the others were getting increasingly anxious. They would carry out their final duties, and then make their attempts at escape. Magda must have already given the children their sleeping potions.

He closed his journal and squared it on the desk. He placed his pen parallel to its spine, then he rose and straightened his jacket. He felt calm. He left the room and wound himself up the spiral staircase to the floor above. The children were almost asleep when he entered. He went to each one and kissed their foreheads. Magda waited nervously by the door, a spoon in her hands.

"Goodnight children."

"Goodnight Father."

52

Franz woke up alone, stiff from sleeping outdoors. He was hungry but there was nothing to eat. He got up and staggered towards the sun. He would find Ariadne. She wanted to leave as much as he did. They would hide in the hotel and when things had settled down they would go to Athens. He had been thinking about it. They would have more opportunities in Athens. It would be easier to get to America from there.

He was trying to remember what Forty-Five had been talking about. There was a piece of paper. Beyond that he drew a blank. He had been so tired he might have dreamed it all. As he made his way over the mountain, a group of women were approaching him like a wind. He could not see them and was not aware of what was happening. They had been drinking all night. They still were.

He heard them first, laughing and shrieking, then he could see them as they came over a bluff. They were dishevelled and half naked, some of them completely naked. They were moving fast, screaming and cackling and swigging from a goatskin bag. As they came closer, he was shocked to see Ariadne among them. He had never known her to get drunk this way. She had always seemed so self-controlled. There were scratches on her breasts and her hair was tangled. She was laughing and weeping hysterically.

The day before she had met a friend who invited her to a village festival in the mountains. It was an annual event and very ancient. This year it was bound to be special as the defeat of Germany seemed inevitable. The local wine up there was known to be strong. Ariadne did not generally go in for this sort of thing. She was not a big drinker and large gatherings made her uncomfortable but she decided to accept on the spur of the moment. It would be good to do something different, the last few years had been so bleak and difficult. She would be someone else for a short while.

They reached the village as evening fell and she soon found herself in the company of other women. It was good to hear real laughter again. The wine was definitely strong. It had a liberating effect that came on quickly. She kept drinking and soon felt a delicious abandon. They all felt that way. It was unspoken. They began to strip off their clothes along with the shackles of civilization. They became ecstatic and tearful. They felt their power as women, full of anger and desire. Men were afraid of them. It added fuel to their lust.

They started to move with no sense of direction, breaking things and people along the way. They had no cares, no memory, no pity. There was no time. When they came upon Franz, they encircled him.

"There's a scarecrow man. A scarecrow man."

The chant passed from mouth to mouth. Their hands were on him, tearing at his clothes, clutching for his face and limbs. His trousers fell to his ankles just as he was stepping back to avoid their onslaught and he tripped up.

It was this stumble that cost him his life. As his head smashed into the rock on the ground behind him, causing a blinding flash, he had one last vision.

An owl stared and blinked.

VH

Also from Recital

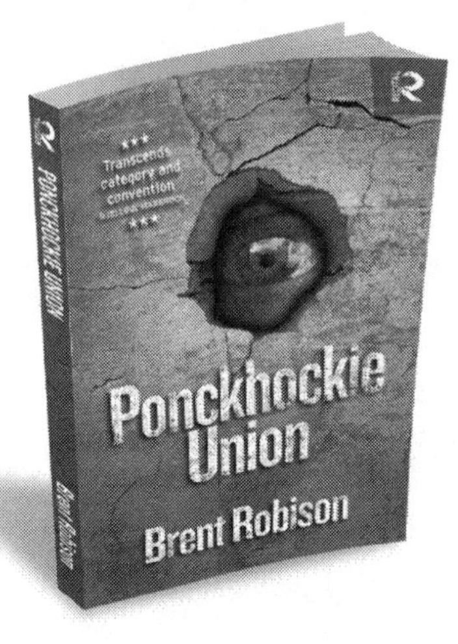

"Ponckhockie Union is an alchemical exploit in which trauma and synchronicity operate as elixirs, ennobling ordinary lives. Its elegant clarity presents two kinds of detective story, one unfolding in the New York's Hudson Valley and the other in the mind of a man who finds his own sense of self getting in the way of his highest aspiration, which is to transcend the world of category and convention and dissolve into the primal material of the cosmos."

Djelloul Marbrook
Award-winning poet/novelist:
Far from Algiers, The Light Piercing Water Trilogy

Sergeant Coot Friedman comes back from the Afghanistan War to an upstate New York village nestled at the foot of a legendary mountain. But for a man with a wayward mind, going home is not easy. He tangles with small town mayhem, certifiably crazy characters, ghosts, visions, and dark forces—both those wearing suits and the more mystical variety. And throughout it all, maintains his taste for good beer.

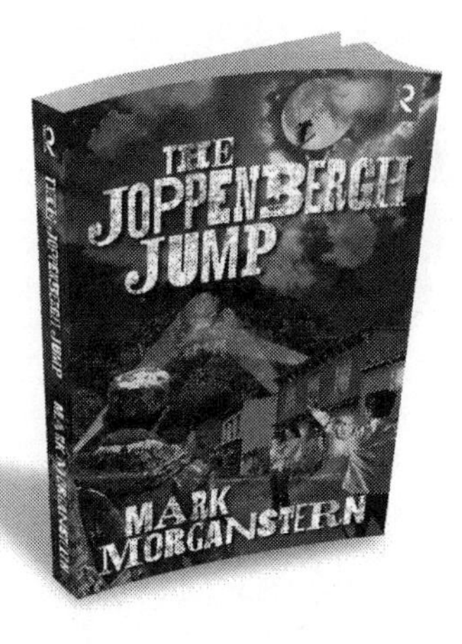

Reweirding the world

www.recitalpublishing.com

Out now in eBook & paperback

Made in the USA
Middletown, DE
20 November 2021

53001496R00144